ANOTHER BIG BUST

By Diane Kelly

Acknowledgements

I have many people to thank for making this book possible. A big thanks to Colene Drace (pictured below) for schooling me in all things biker chick, and answering my questions and then some. You gave me some great ideas for this series! Thanks to my editor Holly Ingraham for your thorough consideration of the draft of this book, and your always helpful feedback and suggestions. Thanks also to my writer friends Becke Turner, Angela Hicks, and Melissa Bourbon for giving me your thoughts on the story as I refined it. Thanks to cover artist Lyndsey Lewellen of Lewellen Designs for crafting such an eye-catching cover for this book. And last but not least, thanks to you wonderful readers who chose this book! I wouldn't have my dream job if it wasn't for you, and I hope you have lots of fun with Officer Shae Sharpe and Deputy Zane Archer.

Chapter One

Swing Shift Surprise

The night was dark, only a sliver of moon in the sky over Durham, North Carolina, but temperatures were pleasant for mid April. My white helmet rested on my head, my clear goggles covered my eyes, and my Harley-Davidson Electra Glide police motorcycle vibrated between my legs as I rode about my beat. The only part of me not jiggling was my breasts. I'd strapped my 38DD's into a zipper-front reinforced sports bra with two-inch wide shoulder straps. The contraption was as tight and confining as a straight jacket—or so I imagined—but it got the job done. I was working the swing shift tonight, and the last thing I needed was my own body getting in the way.

The swing shift ran from 5:00 PM to 2:00 AM. On weekends, the shift was always a busy one for the police department, prime time for bad date drama, bar fights, and drunk drivers. At least the shift was never boring. It would be even more fun if the captain would let me implement the new ideas I'd had for field sobriety tests, including requiring suspects to play a game of Twister. What better way to tell if someone was drunk than by testing their balance, and checking whether they could remember their colors and distinguish between their hands and feet?

My beat, District Four, formed a rough horseshoe shape around an unincorporated area known as Research Triangle Park, home to many pharmaceutical and biomedical research companies. The beat was bordered on the north by the Highway 147, on the west by Chapel Hill, and on the east by Raleigh. On the south, both my beat and the Durham city limits ended at the Chatham County border. Chatham County comprised smaller towns, and was overseen primarily by the sheriff's department rather than municipal police departments.

It was nearing 2:00 AM, with clear skies, only an occasional car on the roads, and just seven minutes left in my shift. Then I could go home to my comfy bed and my condescending cat. I'd tried to take an afternoon nap before my shift but my biorhythms wouldn't have it. At best, I'd dozed for ten minutes or so. Good thing I'd downed a cup of coffee during my midnight break or I'd be too tired to function.

As I motored along the highway, tall, dark forests on both sides, a late flight on approach to the RDU airport raised my gaze to the skies. The plane quickly left my field of vision, but the twinkling stars remained. Though I had zero vocal talent, the beautiful, starry night nonetheless inspired me. "When You Wish Upon a Star" would be the perfect choice, wouldn't it? I opened my mouth to sing, but got only the first word out when—*whap!*—an errant moth entered my throat at 50 mph. The initial sting on impact was bad enough, but now the papery bug was gagging me, too. *Hwak-hwak-hwak!*

I pulled to the side of the road, braked to a stop, and coughed up the moth like my cat coughing up a hairball. Lovely, huh? Such were the hazards of serving as a motorcycle cop, though the situation was far worse for the poor moth than it was for me. A rider expects to get a few bugs in the teeth. Mesmerized by the brilliance of my headlight, the moth had likely had no inkling of its approaching demise. Maybe it had been wishing on a star, too, only the star turned out to be my high-beam. *Rest in peace, little bug.*

I grabbed my water bottle from the holder on my handlebars, slugged back a mouthful, and gargled to loosen any insect remnants. Dispatch came over the radio, summoning officers to a nearby biker bar to break up a fight. *Ugh.* My bed and my cat would have to wait a little longer. No doubt I'd be tied up until well after my shift. But if

I wanted to work regular hours, I should've taken a desk job instead of training to become a police officer. I expelled the water onto the grassy shoulder of the road and pressed the button on my shoulder-mounted radio. "Unit M2 responding."

Lights flashing and siren wailing, I pulled into the dimly lit parking lot of Rockers, a seedy dive named after the British term for motorcycle riders. Rockers sat in an older part of District 4, near an industrial area on the outskirts of town. A row of motorcycles stood in a haphazard line at the front of the lot, while a handful of pickup trucks, SUVs, and cheaper model sports cars were scattered about the parking spot. The place catered to a male customer base, as evidenced by the neon beer signs and the big screen televisions visible through the windows, all tuned to sporting events. A semi-circle of Neanderthals had formed around two bloody men throwing punches at each other in the parking lot. The cavemen cheered them on, hooting and hollering, not one of them making any attempt to stop the carnage. This brawl was their Saturday evening entertainment. Why would they want to stop it?

Leaving my lights flashing, I screeched to a stop, hopped off my bike, and whipped my Taser from my utility belt. I rushed over and stopped just short of the melee. "Break it up!" I shouted. "Now!"

Neither combatant made any attempt to stop fighting, nor did they even glance my way. It was no surprise. After all, my lights and siren had already announced the arrival of law enforcement. If that hadn't been enough to separate the two, it was going to take more drastic measures. Problem was, I couldn't Taser them both at once, and I wasn't sure which of the guys I should target first. I had no idea who'd started the fight, and I didn't want to give either of them an unfair advantage. He might decide to land another punch or a strategic kick while his opponent was being zapped.

I swapped my Taser for my pepper spray, which would render the two similarly incapacitated. *Equal justice.* "Back off!" I hollered, motioning for the crowd to retreat. Just like the brawlers, they ignored me, none wanting to give up the vantage points they'd pushed and shoved each other to attain. Some would become collateral damage but, hey, they'd been warned and would have no one to blame but themselves. Besides, these guys reeked of beer and

B.O. A dose of pepper spray might actually freshen up the parking lot.

My goggles would protect my eyes, but my nose and mouth were exposed. I pressed my lips together, took a deep breath, and held it as I pushed the button. *Psshhhh!* The air filled with an acrid scent and the cries of men who could no longer see or breathe. *Should've backed off like I told you to.*

"Fuck-ck-ck!" one of the fighters cried, his curse descending into a cough that threated to break a few ribs. He wrapped his arms around his torso as if to hold himself together.

The other wailed and summoned mucus up from the deepest depths of his lungs before bending forward with his hands on his knees and spitting the blob out on the pavement with a revolting *splat.*

The one who was coughing seemed more debilitated by the spray, so I figured I had a little more time before he'd come around. I'd take care of the other first. Still holding my breath, I fanned my face, exchanged the spray for a pair of cuffs, and rushed the man who was bent over. I shoved him from behind and he fell forward onto the pavement, skidding on his palms until he fell fully flat, making himself easier for me to handle. Before he could figure out what was happening, I had a knee in his back and his arms yanked up behind him. A couple of *clicks* later and he was cuffed.

He turned his head, scraping his already bloody nose on the pavement, and glared at me with his one visible eye. It was a green eye. A bloodshot and watery eye. *But a familiar eye.* The man's hair was mostly a dull gray now, but it might have once been brown. His left hand bore three circular scars. The scars were familiar, too, the result of a dog bite.

My heart revved to a thousand rpms. *Could it be? After all these years?*

I pushed the sleeve of his T-shirt up for verification. Sure enough, the lecherous cartoon skunk known as Pepé LePew smiled at me from the man's right bicep, a desperate black-and-white female cat caught helplessly in his clutches. The image depicted precisely why I'd become a police officer. To help the helpless, caught up in life's clutches.

The man snarled at me. "You trying to get me naked, Officer Sugar Tits?"

I ground my knee into his back ribs before standing. "That's no way to talk to your daughter."

"Daughter?" He rolled over onto his side and looked up at me, squinting his weepy eyes as if trying to see in me the young girl I'd been the last time he'd laid eyes on me twenty years ago. "Shae?" For just an instant, his surly expression faltered and a surprised smile brightened his face. And, for just that instant, he wasn't the father who'd been an unpredictable powder keg and run out on his family, but the man who'd played tickle monster and Tinkertoys with his young girls, and taken them for rides in the sidecar he'd attached to his Kawasaki, their hands stretched up over their heads as their hair blew back behind them and they cried *"Weee!"* But just as quickly as the smile had come, it was gone. Maybe it had never been there at all, only the hopeful thinking of that now-grown girl wishing on a star. Scowling, he snorted. "You look just like your nagging bitch of a mother."

Nagging bitch? All my mother had ever asked of this man is that he help support the children he'd fathered. If he'd been any kind of man at all, he wouldn't have had to be asked in the first place. He'd contributed little to the family's upkeep, and the only things he'd left me with when he'd gone were his love of motorcycles and his last name, Sharpe. Ironically, he was anything but sharp. Thanks to this worthless jerk, my Mom, my sister, and I been tossed out on the streets.

I combusted with hot fury, my hand going again for my Taser. *I'll show him just how bitchy a woman can be.* I ripped my Taser from my belt and aimed it at him, a red dot of light in the middle of his forehead and another over his cold heart indicating where the prongs would hit him if I deployed the device. It would have given me no end of pleasure to repeatedly zap him until his now-gray hair burst into flame. But summoning every bit of willpower, I stopped myself. To paraphrase lyrics from the popular

8

Police song, my body camera would record every word I'd say, every move I'd make, and every vow I'd break. Unless I wanted to find myself in Internal Affairs facing an excessive force charge, I'd have to keep control of myself. Getting some revenge on my asshole of a father wasn't worth losing my job. Still, if I was a little slow to cuff the other brawler, who could blame me? After all, I was just one cop here, all alone without backup . . .

The other man's coughing began to subside as I returned the Taser to my belt and reached for my second set of cuffs, taking much more time than necessary, feeling around my belt as if I couldn't find them. *Are they over here? No. Here? No. Ah, there they are.* In the meantime, the other guy pulled his leg back and landed a solid kick in my father's kidneys. *Oof!* He curled into a fetal position.

"Enough!" I shouted, secretly thinking *you got exactly what you deserved, you worthless waste of human flesh.*

When my father's sparring partner broke into a fresh round of coughs, I seized his moment of vulnerability to jerk his wrist up behind him and force him up against a nearby car where I could better immobilize him. In seconds, he, too, was cuffed and under control. Luckily for me, backup arrived at that moment to take the two men off my hands.

Driving the cruiser was my closest friend on the force, a female officer named Amberlyn. She threw the gearshift into park and climbed out of her squad car. Her wavy auburn hair was pulled back into a French braid. She was skinny and short, but as scrappy as they come. What she lacked in size she made up for in strength and speed. She and I had gone through the academy together.

After greeting me with a "hey" and a congenial fist bump, Amberlyn pointed a finger at the men. "No shenanigans in my cruiser. Hear me?"

They responded with incoherent grunts and grumbles.

She and I loaded my father and his fellow combatant into the backseat of her cruiser, adding zip ties to their ankles to prevent them from kicking at each other on the drive to lockup. I sent the entourage on their merry way with my promise to get statements from witnesses and run by the station afterward to file a report.

As Amberlyn's cruiser turned out of the parking lot, I ventured a final glance at the man in the backseat, the man I'd once called Daddy. To my surprise, he was looking at me, too. His expression was no longer angry, but resigned. If I didn't know better, I might even say he looked ashamed and remorseful. He blinked, as if to hold back tears, but I knew better. His wet eyes must be merely an aftereffect of the pepper spray.

I turned to the remaining men, who were wiping their eyes and ambling back to the bar. "Stay where you are!" I ordered. "I need to get statements from you."

They responded by muttering curses and skewering me with their glares.

"You," I pointed at the man who'd been cheering the loudest during the fight. "You're up first."

The man took only a couple steps toward me before slipping his thumbs into the front pockets of his jeans, framing his groin with his hands, and rocking back on the heels of his boots. "I ain't seen nothin'."

The others murmured similar statements.

I swung my gaze from one end of the group to the other. "Maybe you'd all remember better if I interviewed you at the station, ran a background check to see if you have outstanding warrants."

The thought of being dragged down to the police station rather than staying here and drinking beer seemed to shut them up. I questioned them briefly one by one. To a man, they all said my father had started the fight by stealing the other man's barstool when he went to the bathroom and refusing to give it up when the man came back. Though the other guy landed the first punch, my father was the first to get physical, poking the other guy in the chest. "He asked for it," one of them said.

Why am I not surprised? I remembered my father coming home all those years ago from his nights out with "the boys." Many times he'd sported a swollen lip, black eye, or bloody nose. I supposed I should be glad he'd never directed his violent tendencies toward my mother, my sister, or me, instead merely neglecting and verbally abusing us. *Thank heaven for small favors.*

By the time I'd gathered the witness statements, returned to the station to type up my report, and driven home, it was well after 3:00 in the morning. Despite the late hour, I sent off a text to Trixie. She took her hearing aids out when she went to bed at night, so the *ping* of my message wouldn't wake her. She'd find it in the morning. *Round up the girls. This chick needs to ride.*

Chapter Two

She'll be Coming 'Round the Mountain

Sunday afternoon, I was riding lead bike as the seventeen women who made up the Dangerous Curves motorcycle club leaned en masse to the left, banking around the final foothill that marked our descent out of the North Carolina Piedmont region. My blond hair billowed out from the bottom of my helmet like a wild bridal veil. Despite the industrial-strength sports bra doing its best to stabilize my chest, my breasts shifted with the change in gravitational and centrifugal forces. Riding a motorcycle involved geometry, engineering, and physics. Fortunately, no actual computations were necessary. Math had never been my thing. A rider simply had to obey these laws of nature to stay in control. Of course experience and practice didn't hurt, either.

The weekend ride on the Blue Ridge Parkway had been both thrilling and therapeutic, just what I'd needed. Friday night's surprise family reunion had dredged up a lot of unresolved hurt and anger, but the feelings had settled down now to a simmering resentment. The mountain air was crisp and clean, cleansing, and the long-range views helped a woman keep things in perspective. Plus, nothing restores a soul like the wind in your hair and the sun on your face.

Beatrix, better known as Trixie, eased up next to me on her touring bike. At 67, she was the matriarch of our bunch, having founded the Dangerous Curves back in the 1970's. Her long, shiny

white braid sparkled in the sun like a unicorn's tail. She rode a
Heritage Classic model in a beautiful blue-green color called
Tahitian Teal. I'd never suffered penis envy, but I would kill to have
a bike like Trixie's between my legs. My silver Harley-Davidson
Street 750 model was far from the flashiest or most expensive
motorcycle of the bunch. In fact, my bike was the most affordable
Harley model available. But that didn't keep me from enjoying it.
Someday, when my savings account allowed, I'd upgrade to a
fancier model.

Passing motorists turned curious heads as the Dangerous
Curves merged onto Interstate 40, heading east. In three hours we'd
be back home in Durham, where we'd disperse until next month's
ride. But now, a *beep-beep* from behind us said that someone needed
a potty, smoke, or coffee break. At the next exit, we took the ramp
and proceeded to a truck stop, where each of the Curves could
indulge as she saw fit.

We lined up our bikes along the side of the building. I lifted
the faceplate of my pink cat-head helmet, which came complete with
pointy ears on top. Two guys wearing faded jeans and flannel shirts
with the sleeves cut out climbed down from a rusty pickup and
glanced my way. Their eyes zeroed in on my breasts, which strained
the fabric of my denim jacket. *Typical.* My bust often rendered men
incapable of coherent thought. *Simple creatures.*

After lingering much too long on my chest, the driver's gaze
moved up to my face, a lustful grin spreading his lips to expose teeth
that would've been at home on a rodent. His eyes flickered to the
feline ears on my helmet. "Nice pussy. I'll give you five bucks to pet
you." He waggled his fingers and thrust his pelvis forward. "We can
see where it goes from there." He and his buddy snickered.

I rolled my eyes, but otherwise ignored them. They were
looking to get a rise out of me. I wasn't about to give them the
satisfaction. You have to choose your battles in life.

As the men headed into the truck stop, Trixie turned to our
fellow Curves, who comprised a varied assortment of shapes, sizes,
and colors. "Fifteen minutes, ladies, and we head back out on the
road."

Murmurs of acknowledgment filled the air, along with the smell of cigarettes being lit up. This being North Carolina, home to Big Tobacco, our group had its fair share of Marlboro ma'ams. Other members of the Curves headed inside to use the facilities or buy a drink or snack. I was among them.

The inside of the truck stop smelled like motor oil and fried foods. I aimed for the refrigerated case at the back to round up a bottle of Cheerwine, a cherry-flavored soda made right here in the state. It might be full of sugar and empty calories, but I'd been raised on the stuff and was hopelessly addicted. Besides, I did Zumba to offset the effects of the sugary soda. *Everyone's entitled to at least one vice, right?* The two men from the parking lot passed me on their way back up the aisle with a six-pack of cheap beer in their hands. They treated me to another lecherous leer.

As I emerged from the store a few minutes later, the men drove away in their pickup. Words written in lipstick on their tailgate announced BIG ASSHOLES WITH TINY DICKS. I recognized the coral shade of the lettering. It was the same color currently tinting Trixie's lips.

I turned to her and she treated me to a broad smile, holding up a tube. "Speak softly and carry a big lipstick."

"I owe you a new tube of Kissable Coral."

She applied a fresh coat to her lips and smacked them. "You owe me nothing, Shae."

Trixie was both a good friend and the grandmother I'd never had. I'd discovered the Dangerous Curves years ago, when they'd met up for a few games at the bowling alley where I'd been slinging beer and nachos in the snack bar. Back then, I'd still been riding the barely street-legal dirt bike I'd bought with my meager earnings. On learning that I, too, was a biker chick, Trixie had invited me to go on a ride with the Curves through the sandhills. She later took me under her wing. In fact, it was Trixie who'd first suggested I apply for the police academy. *"You're the first to step up when any of the gals need help with something,"* she'd said. *"You'd find a career in public service rewarding. Besides, what other job would pay you to ride around on a Harley all day?"* I'd given her words some thought and, a few days later, submitted my application. Luckily for me, the Durham PD didn't require a college degree. I'd been just 21 at the time, but wise for my years. What I lacked in book smarts I more than made up for in street smarts. Yep, I had Trixie to thank for helping me find my purpose in life.

I cut her another grateful glance. "Thanks for organizing the ride today. This is just what I needed."

"Glad I could help," she said. "But you realize this is just a temporary fix, don't you? You're going to have to confront this problem head on."

"I already confronted my problem head on," I said. "Friday night. Filled his sinuses with pepper spray."

She waved a dismissive hand. "I didn't mean your father. I meant your feelings about him."

"Isn't that the same thing?"

"Not at all," she said. "You need to find a way to forgive him so that you can let go of your resentment. If not, it'll just keep festering."

"How am I supposed to forgive someone who just disappeared? Who's never said he's sorry?"

"That makes it harder, for sure," she said. "But have you ever wondered why he abandoned his family? What made him such a lousy father? Your mother must have once saw something good in him, or she wouldn't have fallen in love with him. What went wrong?"

A couple of the Curves walked up, putting an end to our private conversation and leaving me with something to think about. We ladies climbed back onto our bikes, got our motors running, and set back out on the road. Back in Durham, the ladies peeled off one-by-one, or sometimes two-by-two, to return to their homes. I raised a hand in goodbye to Trixie and the remaining Curves as I took the exit for Fayetteville Road.

My home was a first-floor apartment in a mega-sized

complex in the southern part of Durham, relatively close to Southpoint Mall, but not so near that I paid a premium for it. The location was perfect, as it was sat within my beat and had easy access to I-40. I turned into the parking lot and swerved to miss a suicidal squirrel who scampered into my path, an acorn in its teeth. Circling around to the back of the complex, I slowed as I approached my apartment. After cutting the motor, I climbed off my motorcycle, walked the bike to the door of my unit, and rolled it inside, careful to keep the tires on the rubber runners I'd laid down to prevent dirt and oil from marring the carpet in my place. My Harley was my baby. No way would I leave my precious motorcycle outdoors to be subjected to the elements and lookie-loos who couldn't keep their hands to themselves. Ditto for my police motorcycle. The two sat side by side in what would have been a dining room had I owned a table and chairs. I made do with a single barstool at the breakfast bar.

My tuxedo cat padded from the bedroom. I'd taken him in after his former owner abandoned him at the apartment complex along with a broken chair when he'd moved out. He'd been skittish and scrawny, hosting a party for all sorts of parasites when I'd finally caught him. I'd taken him to the vet, nursed him back to health, and named him Oscar in honor of the male celebrities who donned tuxedos and posed on the red carpet before the Academy Awards. The cat cast me a look of utter disgust, and issued an irritated, insistent trill that said, "You're late serving my dinner. Get it *now* or I'll nip your ankles."

I gave the pompous puss a salute. "Yes, sir!"

He proceeded into the small galley kitchen, looking back to make sure I was following him. I retrieved a can of his favorite fishy food, opened it, and upended the can on a saucer. I knelt down and set it on the floor in front of him. "Your order, my lord." As he dug in, I reached out and scratched his head. He growled as he ate, letting me know he was only tolerating my affection because he was too hungry to sink his teeth into my hand. I chuckled and stood. "I love you, too, Oscar."

#

After donning my uniform Monday morning, I twisted my long hair into a low bun on the back of my head, slid my helmet over it, and hopped onto my police bike to swing by the District 4 substation for the 8:00 AM roll call. I was scheduled to work the day shift this week. Not generally as exciting as the swing or night shifts, but much easier to stay awake for.

Our station was supervised by Captain Carter, a fiftyish fireplug who'd blazed trails by becoming one of the first black female SWAT officers in the city years ago. We street cops formed a perimeter around the small conference room. I stood in my usual spot along the back wall beside Amberlyn as Captain Carter briefed us from the podium.

"We've had reports of a group of teenaged girls shoplifting from various stores at Southpoint Mall. Mostly jewelry and accessories, small things they can shove into their purses and pockets. If you're in the area after school hours, run a foot patrol and make your presence known to the shopkeepers and any kids you come across. Let's nip this in the bud. There have also been three reports of classic cars stolen around the city. A 1964 Aston Martin, a '68 Charger, and a 1955 Bel Air. Two classic cars are missing in Raleigh, too. All had been restored. We suspect there's a theft ring targeting valuable older vehicles. Keep an eye out for anything suspicious."

While car theft had been a staple of police work years ago, vehicle theft was less common these days. Many newer cars featured tracking systems, making them riskier targets. Late-model cars also had keyless entry and ignitions, and high-tech skills and devices were necessary to break into them and start the engines. Unlike older cars, more recently manufactured models could not be hot-wired. These facts might be why the thieves had decided to target classic cars rather than newer vehicles. My heart went out the victims. Thanks to an unfortunate series of events in my childhood, I knew what it was like to discover your car missing.

Captain Carter ended the briefing the way she always did, by leading us in an abbreviated pep talk and cheer. That's what happens when your police captain was also once captain of her high school's cheerleading squad. "Who's got the best cops in Durham?" she called.

"District Four!" we called back.

She cupped her hands around her mouth. "I can't hear you!" she hollered. She cupped her hands around her ears now as we shouted, "District Four!"

"You know it!" She took a place by the door, and raised her hand with her thumb tucked in and fingers upright. As we exited the room, she treated each of us to a high four, her special version of a high five for District Four. As her hand met mine, her pointed gaze met my eyes. "Be careful out there, Officer Sharpe."

"I will," I promised. Serving as a motorcycle cop came with some inherent risks not faced by cops in cruisers. What might only be a fender-bender for a squad car could be a fatality on a bike. I'd have no vehicle to shield me should I end up in a shootout, either. Still, I wouldn't trade the freedom of roaming the beat on my bike for anything.

Out in the parking lot, I donned my helmet, climbed onto my bike, and headed off to patrol my beat. As a motorcycle cop, I was not equipped to transport suspects, which left me handling a disproportionate share of traffic matters, noise complaints, and alarm calls, most of which turned out to be false alarms. At this time of the morning, with rush hour at its peak along I-40, traffic mostly regulated itself. Not easy to speed when you had a wall of cars doing a mere 20 mph in front of you. Rather than waste my time on the freeway, I headed over to the local high school. Between the number of kids walking to school and the inexperienced teen drivers behind the wheel of many of the cars, the school zone could be a dangerous place. Still, I wasn't one of those cops who lay in wait, trying to catch someone screwing up so I could issue them an expensive ticket. I preferred to sit out in the open, my presence a deterrent to bad driving and a way to keep everyone safe and encourage good habits.

I parked my bike near the main entrance to the school parking lot, where I could keep an eye on the traffic approaching from both directions. I pulled my bullhorn from my saddle bag and rested in on my thigh. A golden yellow school bus lumbered up the road, creaking on its chassis and spewing exhaust as it passed me to turn into the bus-only lane farther down. A teen girl driving a beat-up Subaru cut the turn too close and rolled up on the curb for a second or two before the car bumped back down onto the asphalt. She cast a nervous glance in my direction. I smiled to relieve her anxiety and motioned with my hand for her to continue. *No harm, no foul, no ticket.*

A harried mother who didn't see me swung into the oncoming lane to circle around the cars turning into the lot. She slammed on her brakes when she spotted me, her two children rocking forward in their seats. I raised my bullhorn to my lips and pressed the button. "Take it easy, Mom!"

She raised contrite shoulders and mouthed the word "sorry!" through the windshield.

Two minutes before the bell was scheduled to ring, both foot and road traffic had dwindled to a trickle. A skinny girl came sprinting up the sidewalk, hanging on tight to the backpack flapping against her shoulders. Just after she cleared the crosswalk, a boy in a sporty red Mitsubishi 3000GT squealed around the corner.

I reached out, switched on my lights, and started my motor. The boy's eyes met mine through the glass, only the word he mouthed wasn't *sorry*. It was the F-bomb. I followed after him as he pulled into the parking lot. He eased over to the curb by the gymnasium and I climbed off my bike.

He unrolled his window and rested his arm on the ledge. He wore a letterman jacket. Football. A patch on the arm identified him as an all-state quarterback.

I stepped up to his door. "License and insurance."

He pointed to the school building. "It's only a minute until the bell. How about you do me a solid and let me off with a warning?" He cocked his head, batted his green eyes, and flashed me his best smile, as if a gander at his perfectly straight pearly whites was going to get him out of trouble.

"That face might work for your mother and the girls in your class, but it doesn't work for me." Though I was tempted to take him down a peg or two, life would teach this kid soon enough that, while he might be a big fish in a small pond today, his pretty face and ability to handle a pigskin would only get him so far. "How about you show me your license and insurance like I asked, kiddo?"

Sighing, he rummaged around in his glove box and wallet before handing me the requested documentation.

I took the paperwork from him. Everything appeared to be in order. A search in the system indicated he had no prior traffic citations. "What's your hurry this morning?"

"I overslept." He pulled a piece of paper from his backpack. "I was up until midnight working on this. It's impossible!"

I looked over the homework handout. It was all X's and Y's and numbers and parentheses. "Algebra?"

He nodded and grimaced. "It's kicking my butt."

"It kicked mine, too." I handed his paperwork and homework back to him. "Those math problems are punishment enough. But slow down. You're not just endangering yourself, you're endangering others. Next time I won't go easy on you."

"Thanks!"

An hour later, I was riding north on state highway 751, my view obscured by the delivery truck in front of me, when dispatch came over the radio to announce a vehicle theft, what we beat cops referred to as a rollin' stolen. "Be on the lookout for a 1970 lime green Plymouth Barracuda. The car was just taken from the Duke Health Center parking lot. License plate is DV CUDA."

The fact that the license plate number included the letters DV meant that the vehicle was owned by a disabled veteran. It was bad enough someone had stolen a car, but to take it from someone who'd been injured in war? That was especially low.

While a lot of crime happened at night while people slept, a surprising amount happened in broad daylight. Residential burglaries were common mid-day. Few people were at home to witness the crimes or, if they were home, they weren't looking out their windows where they might spot a thief. Muggings in busy parking lots happened during the daylight hours, too. Still, it was a bold move to snatch such a brightly painted vehicle in the daytime from a public parking lot. The thief must really want the car to take such chances. A lime green Barracuda would be like a neon light going down the road.

Holy crap! There it is now!

Chapter Three

The Buck Stops Here

The green Barracuda passed me, heading south. The delivery truck in front of me had obscured my view, and I hadn't spotted the car until it was right on me. By the time it registered in my brain that it was the stolen car, it was a hundred yards behind me, too late for me to get a look at the driver.

I slowed, waited for three more oncoming cars to pass—*hurry up, slowpokes!*—and hooked a tight U-turn, putting a leg out to steady myself. I flipped on my lights and headed after the muscle car. I thumbed the button on my handlebars to activate the mic attached to my helmet. "I've got eyes on the Barracuda. Heading south on 751 approaching Stagecoach Road. Unit M2 in pursuit."

Three cars separated me from the Barracuda. The person driving the SUV in front of me eased over to the right and I cranked my wrist back, gunning my engine to pass. The man driving the next car that stood between me and my quarry was looking down at his cell phone, weaving back and forth in his lane, totally oblivious to my presence. *Sheesh!* I flipped on my siren—*WOO-WOO*—and he reflexively tossed his phone into the air and hit his brakes in response. Luckily, I'd anticipated his moves and had put more space between us. He eased over, too, and I sped past him. The final vehicle began to move over as we came upon Stagecoach Road, and I pulled up beside it to pass. Tires squealing and burning rubber as it fishtailed, the Barracuda turned onto Stagecoach. Once the car gained purchase, it roared and took off at warp speed, leaving an acrid-smelling cloud of dust and smoke in its wake.

"He's making a run for it!" I hollered into my mic.

Argh! The turn was blocked by the final vehicle, preventing me from following the stolen car and forcing me to continue down 751. As soon as I could, I whipped another U-turn and headed back to Stagecoach, my siren *woo-woo-wooing* all the while.

I vectored off for the turn and pulled back on the accelerator, my bike rocketing forward as I straightened out. I leaned forward for better aerodynamics, my boobs brushing the fuel tank in front of the seat. The Barracuda had a good lead on me now and was nowhere in sight. While I normally loved the lush woods that covered the Raleigh-Durham region, today the trees were a nuisance, limiting my view. This chase would've been easier if the landscape were clear and open, like a Texas plain or an Arizona desert.

The area quickly became rural as it approached Jordan Lake, the road littered with dry pine needles and the spiky balls that fell from the Sweetgum trees. I rode as fast as I dared, knowing deer occasionally darted across the roadways here. A deer was dangerous enough to the occupants of a car, but a run-in could easily be deadly for someone on a motorcycle.

I was passing the cutoff for Farrington Mill Road, when I glanced to the left and spotted the back bumper of the Barracuda disappear around a bend a quarter mile down. Once again I slowed and whipped a U-turn to continue my pursuit. Seconds later, I passed the sign marking the end of the the Durham city and county limits. I radioed my current position to dispatch. "Get me backup from Chatham County!" I was in the sheriff department's territory now. It was only polite to invite them to the party.

A minute later, a large white SUV approached from the other direction. The Chevy Tahoe sported black and burgundy stripes and the sheriff's department gold star, the lights on top twirling and twinkling. Surely the deputy hadn't inadvertently passed the Barracuda. The bright green paint job would be impossible to miss. *Has the car turned off somewhere into the woods?*

I was slowing to rendezvous with the deputy when movement on the edge of the woods ahead caught my eye. An enormous buck strode out of the trees. The area's deer had recently undergone their annual antler shedding, but this buck already sported a surprisingly well-developed set of new velvet-covered nubs. It looked as if two gnarled hands were reaching up from the top of his head, both of them extending the middle finger in a rude gesture. *Buck you.* The big beast would likely be a twelve-point buck come fall.

I slowed a little to give him time to finish crossing the road. But instead, he stopped on the road, his long body blocking the entire lane. He turned his head to face me and raised his chin in challenge.

NOOO!

I braked as hard as I dared and whipped my handlebars. But I'd whipped them too far too fast. Physics kicked in, taking my bike down onto its side and pulling me with it. Momentum carried my motorcycle over the damp dead leaves and pine needles along the shoulder. As I slid along the shoulder, hanging onto my bike for dear life, I prayed I wouldn't hit a tree become roadkill.

Either the gods or my guardian angel must have been looking out for me. I slid to a stop, lying on my side atop the damp, natural debris that had broken my fall and absorbed my energy. My bike remained clenched between my thighs as my heart pounded like a piston in my chest and my blood roared in my ears like wild water rapids. The buck trotted safely across as the SUV rolled up on the opposite shoulder. The deer stopped at the edge of the woods and looked back at me as if to say *These woods belong to me and don't you forget it.*

A deputy leapt from the vehicle. He wore black pants and a tan shirt paired with a black tie and campaign hat. Leaving his door open, he rushed across the road, his face in shadow from both the shady woods and the brim of his hat. "Sweet Jesus! Are you all right?"

By then, I was leveraging my bike to a stand. I toed the kick stand to hold it up and took stock of myself and my motorcycle.

Miraculously, other than some smudges of moist dirt and leaves, neither seemed worse for the wear. Sliding across the ground had given me a minor wedgie, though. I glanced up at the deputy for the first time, and felt a hot buzz rocket through my system. Fortunately, this hot buzz was far more pleasant than the one I'd experienced during the police academy, when our training officer had given us a zap with a Taser so we could experience firsthand the power of the weapon. I reached up, pulled off my helmet, and shook out my hair. "I'm fine."

His jaw dropped. "You're a woman?"

Clearly, he hadn't gotten a good look at me before. I hadn't gotten a good look at him, either. We'd both been too agitated, moving too fast. I removed my goggles and replied, "One-hundred-percent biker chick."

He stopped gaping and stood up taller. "Sorry. I've just never met a female motorcycle cop before."

The deputy had removed his hat and tucked it under his arm. Like the graceful yet homicidal deer, the officer had broad shoulders, long legs, and a natural athletic masculinity. He also had deep brown eyes with gorgeous bronze flecks. *I could stare into these eyes forever.* To his credit, his eyes were focused on my face, not my chest. Being a total hypocrite, I shifted my attention from his chiseled facial features to his firm pectoral muscles, which were at eye level with me. *How tall is this guy? Six-feet-two? Three?* The name tag positioned over his left pec read ARCHER. Lest my sudden surge of lust be obvious, I looked down again and brushed the dirt off my uniform. "Did you see the Barracuda, Deputy Archer?"

"No," he said. "It must have turned off somewhere before we met up. All I saw was that big buck until I saw you. Come fall, he'll have quite a nice rack."

I'd been told more times than I could count what a *nice rack* I had. Seeming to realize he'd uttered an unintended sexual blunder, the deputy averted his eyes and pulled his radio from his belt to contact dispatch. "We need available units to scour the area around Farrington Mill and Farrington Point Roads," he said. "Be on the lookout for the green Barracuda. Can we get a chopper in the air, too?"

Dispatch came back a few seconds later. "The chopper's on its way."

With any luck, the helicopter or one of the other deputies would spot the car and the driver would be taken into custody.

Deputy Archer gestured to the shoulder beside us where I'd wiped out. "That was an impressive move. Did you slide like that on purpose?"

I snorted. "Nobody lays their bike down on purpose, trust me. If they tell you they meant to do it, they're lying."

He cocked his head, a grin tugging at his lips. "So I shouldn't be impressed then?"

"Oh, you should be impressed," I said, brushing off my badge. "But not by that."

The grin spread his lips into a smile, and damn if it wasn't a sexy one.

I looked off down the road. "My captain told us in roll call that there's been a rash of classic cars stolen in Durham and Raleigh recently."

The deputy's head bobbed in acknowledgement. "Seems I heard something about that."

I thought aloud. "I wonder if the thieves have been taking these back roads on their way to South Carolina, or maybe even farther south to Florida or Georgia."

"Could be," he agreed. "Cutting through here would be a good way to avoid the freeways and interstates where they're more likely to get caught."

Automated license plate readers had been installed along many of the major arteries and were a useful tool for law enforcement in tracking vehicles, but the cost of the systems meant they couldn't be put in place along all roadways. They were rarely used in rural areas.

Still, while automated trackers were likely rare in Chatham County, the sheriff's department would have plenty of officers on the roads who might have noticed something, including the deputy standing before me. "Have you noticed an unusual number of classic cars coming through the county recently?"

"Can't say that I have. Don't recall any of the other deputies mentioning it, either."

I mulled things over some more. It was possible, maybe even likely, that the thief driving the Barracuda had come this way only because I was in pursuit and turning on Stagecoach Road had seemed to offer the best chance of escape. He could have ended up in Chatham County by pure happenstance, rather than because of a preconceived plan.

A *whup-whup-whup* told us the helicopter was approaching. Our gazes shifted to watch the chopper as it stopped and hovered farther down the road, high enough that it should be able to see for a good distance on a clear day like today.

A voice came over Deputy Archer's radio, probably the chopper's co-pilot as the pilot would be busy operating the aircraft. "We're not seeing a green Barracuda. Which way did you say it went again?"

"South, as far as we know," the deputy replied.

"Ten-four."

The chopper made a small circle and banked to head in the other direction, gaining altitude as it went, probably to give the two men inside a wide view of the roads. We waited a minute or two in anticipation, expecting the pilot to report a sighting at any moment.

When no word came in, Archer frowned and tried his radio again, speaking to the guys in the chopper. "You boys in the air got anything?"

A voice came back. "Yeah. Squat."

The deputy exhaled sharply in frustration. "The thief couldn't have just disappeared into thin air."

Or could he? I glanced around at the thick woods, thinking how easy it would be to conceal a stolen car among the trees where even a helicopter or camera-mounted drone wouldn't be able to see through the canopy of leaves. We'd assumed the car thief would still be on the move along one of the county roadways, but maybe we were wrong. "Maybe the thief ditched the car around here somewhere."

"If that's the case," Deputy Archer said, arching a brow and giving me a pointed look, "that means this is a matter for the Chatham County Sheriff's Department."

"Not necessarily," I countered. "We Durham cops gets dibs on anyone nabbed in a hot pursuit."

"True, but only if you catch them." He rocked back on his heels and raised his hands palms up. "You didn't catch anyone."

I narrowed my eyes at him. "Touché." Okay, so I wouldn't get credit for an arrest made by the sheriff's department. That was all right with me. I wasn't in the law enforcement game for gold stars. I was in it to prevent people from doing other people wrong, and to make the bad guys pay when they did. I'd seen my mother done wrong, more than once and by more than one person. I'd do what I could to keep someone else from suffering the way she had.

I gestured to his radio. "Ask if they see anyone walking on a roadside." If the thief had ditched the car in the woods, it was possible he was making an escape on foot.

Archer repeated my question over the airwaves. "See anyone walking on a roadside?"

The voice from the chopper came back again. "All we see are some guys launching a fishing boat at the lake, golfers on the greens at the Governors Club, and trees, trees, and more trees." In other words, the usual sights.

Archer's gaze assessed me as I clipped my helmet onto my

bike and wrangled my loose locks back into submission in a messy bun. "You mentioned other stolen cars. What makes and models?"

I racked my brain. "An Aston Martin, a Bel Air, and a Chevy Charger. Can't remember what year models exactly, but all were before 1970."

He nodded. "I'll spread the word, tell everyone to keep an eye out."

"We'd appreciate it."

"In the meantime," he said, "I'll escort you back to the Durham County Line."

I donned my goggles and helmet again, and slid him some side eye. "I can find it on my own."

"No doubt," he said. "I just want to make sure you know your place."

Know my place? I was about to tell the guy off when I noticed the mischievous gleam in his eyes. *He's only teasing me.* No need to get my panties in any more of a wad than they were already in.

I climbed onto my bike. "Take care, Deputy Archer."

"You, too, Officer Sharpe."

A-ha! So he had looked at my chest. Or my nametag, at least.

As Deputy Archer returned to his SUV and climbed inside, I started my motor and made a slow and careful turn to head back to Durham. True to his word, the deputy followed me back to the county line, giving me a short blast of his siren in goodbye. I returned the sentiment with a raised hand and a couple toots of my bike horn. *Beep-beep!*

Chapter Four

Victim Statement

I checked with dispatch and got the phone number for the car's owner so I could meet up with them and take a statement to include in my report.

A woman answered when I called. I explained who I was, and asked, "Are you back at home?"

"No," she said. "We've been waiting at the medical center. We hoped y'all would catch the thief and bring our car back to us."

I cringed. Victims sometimes expected quick resolutions, but real-life law enforcement moved much slower than in TV and movies. "We did our best," I told her. I'd risked my life, in fact. But no sense whining about it. "The car seems to have disappeared in the woods. Even the chopper couldn't spot it."

"Y'all sent a helicopter up?"

"We did." I didn't mention that it was a Chatham County Sheriff's Department chopper. They'd likely be stealing credit for busting the car thief soon enough, despite the fact that I'd chased him into their hands. Why not let my department enjoy some credit? "Can I come get a statement from you?"

"Of course," she said. "We're on the bench by the doors."

"I'll head right over."

A few minutes later, I pulled my motorcycle into the medical center parking lot. An elderly black man and woman sat on a bench by the automatic doors that led into the building. The man wore khaki pants and a T-shirt bearing the U.S. Marine Corps logo. His face sagged. Ditto for his wife's. She wore slacks and a pink sweater set and clutched a small purse in her hands. Twin walkers stood in front of them.

I parked my bike in an empty spot and approached them, extending my hand. "Good morning. I'm Officer Shae Sharpe."

They stood and shook my hand.

"Jerry Beaumont," the man said by way of introduction.

"I'm Gilda," the woman added.

I whipped out my note pad and took a seat on the bench beside them. "Can you tell me what happened?"

Gilda glanced at her husband and patted his hand. "I'll tell her, dear." She faced me, her forehead lined with worry. "We just had a visit with his cardiologist. It's best if he stays calm."

Jerry chuffed. "Someone stole my car and I'm supposed to stay calm?"

Gilda cast an anxious glance at her husband before turning back to me. "That car was his baby."

"Bought it brand new," Jerry added proudly, staring off in the distance as if visualizing the moment he'd purchased the car all those years ago. "Right off the showroom floor. We'd scrimped and saved for years to get it. I'll never forget the feeling when that salesman put the keys in my hand. I kept it in pristine condition, too. Washed and waxed it regular, kept the chrome shined. When the upholstery showed signs of wear and tear, I had the seats recovered. Same for the dashboard. The interior was immaculate."

"He even found a lime-green tire gauge that matched the paint." Gilda glanced over at her husband and offered a sad smile.

"We had to sell the car in ninety-two. Jerry came back from Desert Storm with a bum leg and two bullets in him. The bullets were too close to his organs for the surgeons to safely remove them. He got a medical discharge from the Marine Corps, but it took a while for the disability benefits to kick in, and they weren't nearly as much as he was earning beforehand. I had to take time off from my job to care for Jerry while he went through physical therapy and recovered. The only way we could make ends meet was to sell the Barracuda."

Jerry shook his head. "Worst day of my life."

That was saying a lot considering he'd been shot and rendered lame in a war.

Gilda patted his hand again before returning her attention to me. "Eventually, when things settled down and we got our finances sorted out, we contacted the car collector we'd sold it to. Once we'd told him our story, he agreed to sell it back to us."

"For three grand more than he'd paid us for it," Jerry muttered. "He'd put a bunch more miles on it, too."

"Look on the bright side, honey," she told him. "At least the Barracuda was ours again."

He threw up his hands. "And now it's gone! Who knows if we'll ever find it."

Gilda slumped, defeated. Tears filled her eyes and her lips quivered. "This couldn't have happened at a worse time. We just got some bad news from the doctor. The lead from the bullets are causing some trouble, and Jerry's ticker's getting worse."

He looked at me, his eyes dark with despair. "I probably won't see that car again before I die. The odds aren't good, are they?"

"I'm so sorry." I didn't want to lie to the man, but I didn't want to give him false hope, either. The other stolen classics hadn't been located, and we had no real leads other than the location where the Barracuda had last been seen. My heart twisted inside my chest. The car thief hadn't just taken a piece of property, he'd taken Jerry's sense of self worth, a primary source of pride and joy for a sick man whose remaining days on earth could be numbered. *I'll find the missing Barracuda if it's the last thing I do.* "I can't promise we'll find your car, but I promise I'll do everything in my power to make that happen. Okay?"

He nodded and his wife offered a weak smile. "That's all we can ask."

I readied my pen. "What time did y'all arrive here?"

"Jerry's appointment was at ten-thirty," Gilda said. "We got here about fifteen minutes early."

I jotted the time on my pad. "Any idea who might have taken the car?"

The two shook their heads. "No idea at all," Jerry said.

"Does anyone else have keys to the vehicle?"

"No." Jerry reached into his pocket and pulled out a key ring, holding it up for me to see. "I've got my key here and Gilda's got the only spare."

His wife reached into her purse and pulled out her keys, holding them up as well. Looked like I could rule out stolen keys.

"Where do you normally park your car at your house?" I asked. "In the garage, driveway, or street?"

"In the garage," Jerry said. "Covered by a custom tarp."

That car really is his baby. "So the car's not normally outside at your house where people can see it."

"No."

I mused aloud. "Since you kept the car out of sight and not easily accessible at your house, I'm thinking whoever targeted the car must have first seen it when you had it out in public. They might have been keeping an eye on your place and followed you here where they could take it without having to break into your garage to get it."

The couple exchanged nervous glances before Gilda looked back at me. "You think someone's been watching us? Watching our house?"

"I don't know for certain," I said. "I'm just saying it's possible. It's also possible the car thief is an opportunist who drives around parking lots looking for targets. There's been five other classic cars stolen in the area recently. It might be a ring."

"Goodness!" Gilda said. "I wish we'd known. We would've driven my Chrysler here instead of the Barracuda."

"Two of the car thefts were in Raleigh," I said. "We're just now piecing things together." Unfortunately, law enforcement only became aware of trends once enough victims had surfaced that the trend could be identified. "Did you notice anyone who seemed to be trailing you here? Or anyone eyeing the car after you arrived?"

"No," Jerry said.

"Me, neither," Gilda added.

"What about someone casing your house? Cruising by multiple times? Maybe jogging or walking past and checking things out?"

"Not that I've noticed," Jerry said.

"I haven't spotted anyone suspicious, either," said Gilda. "Of course, we're not out front too often other than when we're coming and going or getting the mail. We spend most of our time inside or on the screened porch out back when the weather permits."

"Do you have security cameras on your house?"

"No," Gilda said. "We didn't see any real need for them. We've got two big dogs who bark a lot and would discourage anyone from breaking in."

I jotted some notes and asked. "Is there anyone who's shown particular interest in the car?"

Jerry and Gilda exchanged another glance before Jerry spoke. "Our neighbor's teenaged son got his license a few months ago. He asked me if he could take the 'Cuda out for a spin. I told him the only person I let drive it other than myself was my wife. He seemed so disappointed I offered to take him for a ride in it. We rode around for over an hour. He loved it, kept commenting on how 'cool' the car was."

"Does he seem like the kind of kid who might steal a car?"

Jerry shrugged. "Hard to say. He seems responsible enough. He mows lawns for a lot of the folks in the neighborhood in the summers, rakes leaves in the fall. His parents are divorced. His mother's not around much, but I see boys coming and going from their house at all hours. They sometimes shoot hoops in the driveway, get a little rowdy, play their music too loud. But we can't fault him too much. Our own boys did the same when they were that age."

My teenaged half-brother could get loud and rowdy, too, though he preferred video games to sports. "What's the neighbor boy's name and address?"

Jerry said the boy was Brody Riddle. He gave me the boy's address, too. "He lives directly across the street from us. Green house with the dogwood trees out front."

"Got it," I said, making a note on my pad. While it was a school day, Brody could have skipped, or maybe faked an illness so that his mother would have let him stay home. I looked up again. "Anyone else?"

"This might be nothing," Jerry said, "but I went to a classic car rally in Charlotte back in January. They call it 'Cars and Coffee.' It's held the third Saturday of every month from seven to ten in the morning. It's a free event. Everyone just pulls up in the parking lot in their cars and shows 'em off. You get hot rods, muscle cars, sometimes a tricked-out low-rider or two. Anyway, there was a guy there who came over and talked to me for a few minutes. White fella. Introduced himself, asked about the car. He asked to see the inside and he seemed harmless, so I let him sit in the driver's seat and take a look around."

"Do you remember his name?"

"No," he said. "It didn't seem all that important at the time. But I do recall that he had a bushy beard and dark hair. He was wearing a ball cap and mirrored sunglasses, so I can't tell you what color his eyes were or anything like that."

"What about his build?"

"Seemed pretty average all around. I don't remember anything standing out."

"Did he say where he was from?"

"Not that I remember. I didn't ask. I think he might have asked me, though. I vaguely remember talking about the drive down to Charlotte, that awful construction on Interstate Eighty-Five."

"It's a mess," I agreed. I'd been down to the speedway myself for the Outlaw Drag Wars, when novice racers were allowed on the track. One of the other Durham motorcycle cops raced his bike there. I'd had a blast. "Is there anyone who might be able to identify the guy you talked to? Did he have a car there?"

"I don't believe he had a car at the event," Jerry said, "but I can't say for sure. I'm not well connected in the classic car circles. I drove down with a friend. It was the first time we'd done anything like that. We went on a whim after seeing something about it on the internet."

I jotted some notes. *Average build. Hat. Sunglasses. Dark hair. Bushy beard.* It wouldn't surprise me if the thieves tried to change the car up to hide the fact that it was stolen. It wouldn't be hard or costly to swap out hubcaps or tires, or add stripes to the paint or even fully repaint the exterior. But they'd likely leave the interior alone if it was in good shape, as Jerry had mentioned.

My note-taking complete, I slide the pad into the breast pocket of my uniform. "You two got someone to give you a ride home?"

Gilda frowned. "I hate to interrupt our sons or neighbors at work. I suppose we could figure out the bus routes or call a cab.

We've never used Uber. Don't know the first thing about it."

I raised a finger. "Let me see what I can do." I pulled my radio from my pocket and asked whether there was an available officer in the area who could run a courtesy transport.

Amberlyn's voice came back over the airwaves. "Be right there."

I clipped the radio back on my belt. "Your ride will be here shortly."

While we waited for Amberlyn, I told them I'd ask around the medical center, see if anyone saw anything. "Maybe someone happened to see something out the window. I'll check with security, too, see if we can get their video footage."

"Thanks, Officer Sharpe," Jerry said. "If you can get that car back, it'll mean the world to me."

It would mean the world to me, too. "A detective will be in touch with you in the next day or so. In the meantime, law enforcement will keep an eye out for the Barracuda. I've spoken directly with the Chatham County Sheriff's Department, and Durham PD has issued an alert to all jurisdictions in a hundred-mile radius."

Amberlyn rolled up shortly thereafter and climbed out of her cruiser. "Hello, folks."

"Hey, Cass." I introduced her to the Beaumonts.

Gilda took Amberlyn's hand in hers and patted the top of it. "Thanks for the chauffeur service."

Amberlyn smiled. "My pleasure."

I gave Amberlyn a quick rundown of the car theft. "Please keep an eye out and spread the word."

She nodded. "I sure will."

I opened the passenger and back doors for the Beaumonts.

Jerry cut his wife a look. "What will the neighbors think when we show up in a cop car?"

Gilda smiled. "They'll think these old folks finally did something interesting."

His mouth curved in a hint of a smile.

As Jerry climbed into the front and Gilda eased into the backseat, Amberlyn and I collapsed their walkers and loaded them into the trunk. She held out her hand for a fist bump. "Later, 'gator."

I closed my hand and bumped my knuckles against hers. "See ya."

Once they'd driven off, I went into the building and asked the custodian mopping the lobby if there was an on-site management office.

He pointed down the wing to his right. "At the end past the restrooms."

"Thanks."

I headed down the hall and stopped at the last door. Through the narrow glass panel, I could see a woman sitting at a desk inside the small space. I rapped on the glass—*thunk, thunk, thunk.* She looked up and buzzed me in. As I entered, she stood to greet me, her face tightening with concern. "Is something going on?"

"A car was stolen out front earlier."

"Was anyone hurt?"

"No," I said. "The car was taken while the owners were at a doctor's appointment in the building."

She exhaled in relief. "Thank goodness."

"Could I take a look at your security feeds?"

"Of course."

She offered me a folding chair and I scooted it up next to

hers as she logged into the system. She tapped a few keys and swiveled her mouse to bring the footage up on the screen. "What time should I start the feed?"

"Ten minutes after ten," I told her.

"All right." She clicked on a box that showed the time and typed in 10:10 AM. Another click and the feed began rolling. Unfortunately, the video quality wasn't great, the image grainy, but maybe I could still glean something from it.

At 10:13, the green Barracuda rolled up and pulled into one of the designated handicapped parking spots. Jerry climbed out of the driver's side, putting a hand on top of the car to steady himself as he circled around to the back. There, he put a key into the lock and opened the trunk. Had I not spent three weeks of my childhood living in a 1978 Pontiac Safari Station Wagon, I might not have known that older cars came with two different keys, one for the ignition and another for the doors and trunk.

Jerry pulled his and Gilda's walkers from the trunk, opened one of them up, and used it to balance himself as he shuffled up to Gilda's door. He helped her out and she grabbed a hold of the walker. Putting his hand atop the car again, he circled back and unfolded his own walker before closing the trunk. The two then made their way into the medical center, side by side.

A moment later, a white guy appeared at the back of the parking lot, emerging from between two bushes. He weaved through the parked vehicles as he approached the Barracuda. The guy wore an athletic suit in blue and white, the colors of Durham's Duke University, along with a ball cap and mirrored sunglasses. His face was further hidden by a full beard. A backpack was slung over one shoulder. After taking a quick glance around to make sure nobody was watching him, he stepped over to driver's window. He pulled a metal Slim Jim tool from his backpack and slid the metal shaft down into the door at the base of the window. Two wiggles and one pull later, he got the door open. He slid into the car and closed the door, no longer visible on the screen. A mere forty-three seconds later, the car's reverse lights came on. *This guy's a pro.* He backed out of the parking space and drove off.

I asked the woman to forward to a time shortly before the Beaumonts had dialed 9-1-1 to report the theft. The screen showed the couple hobbling out of the building. From the camera's vantage point behind them, we couldn't see their faces. They stopped moving when they noticed the car was no longer in the handicapped spot. They turned their heads to speak to each other, eyes wide and mouths gaping in shock and dismay. Jerry threw his hands into the air and then put them to his head. When he lost his balance and began to fall, he grabbed the handles of his walker to steady himself. Gilda pulled her cell phone from her purse to call the police. All Jerry could do at that point was stare helplessly at the empty parking spot.

The other outdoor cameras provided only a glimpse of the Barracuda driving into and out of the lot. The man did not appear on the indoor feeds.

The woman pulled a thumb drive from her desk. "I can copy the footage for you if you'd like."

"I'd appreciate that," I told her. "The detective assigned to the case will want to review it. But please retain the original video on your system, too."

"No problem." She copied the video and handed me the thumb drive, along with her business card.

After making the rounds of the medical offices, questioning the available staff, and leaving my contact information with each office, I went back outside and glanced around. There were a few other small businesses nearby. I checked in with them, but none had exterior security cameras, only interior units. Having done what I could at the crime scene, I returned to the station. I gave Captain Carter both the drive and a rundown on my pursuit of the stolen car and interview of the victims. I left out the part where the buck nearly killed me. No one likes a whiner.

"Good work, Officer Sharpe," the captain said. "I'll assign the case to a detective this afternoon."

I spent the rest of the day handling traffic matters. Issuing speeding tickets on the interstate. Directing cars around a fender bender near the mall. Citing a semi that was bellowing black smoke. And thinking about Deputy Archer's gorgeous brown eyes.

Chapter Five

Family Dinner

Near the end of my shift, I rode my bike to the address the Beaumonts had given me for Brody Riddle. Four teenaged boys ran about the driveway, playing a game of two-on-two basketball that involved a lot of illegal shoving and unsportsmanlike conduct. As I pulled to the curb and cut my motor, they turned to look at me.

I removed my goggles from my eyes and said, "Which one of you is Brody Riddle?"

A tall, skinny boy with light skin and dark hair raised his hand. He didn't look much like the guy in the video from the medical center. Brody seemed taller and thinner than the guy who'd stolen the car, and sported only sparse, patchy facial hair. Still, the athletic suit might have made his body look fuller, and he could have worn a fake beard. I'd seen all kinds of costume beards for sale at the Halloween store last year. Long, silver wizard beards. Burly black lumberjack beards. A brown Jesus beard. Even a glue-on goatee.

I jerked my head in a *come-here* motion. "Let's talk."

Brody bounced the basketball to his friends and strode over, looking confused but not apprehensive. If he'd stolen the Beaumonts' car, he'd look a little more anxious, wouldn't he? Then again, some criminals were good at hiding their emotions, especially the sociopaths who seemed to experience very little emotion to begin with.

No sense easing him in. I cut right to the chase to see how he would respond to a direct confrontation. "Did you take Jerry Beaumont's Barracuda for a joyride this morning?"

His face grew tighter as his confusion seemed to increase. "No. Mr. Beaumont has taken me for rides before, but today was a school day."

"The car was stolen," I clarified. "You know anything about that?"

"Wait. What?" He looked not only confused now, but distraught. His mouth gaped and his posture went rigid. "Someone took Mr. Beaumont's car?"

"Yes. It was stolen this morning."

"But Mr. Beaumont fought in wars and stuff. He even got shot! It would be really shitty to steal a car from someone like that."

"Agreed. You know how to hot-wire a car?"

"Hot-wire? Isn't that a website for hotels?"

The kid was clueless. He didn't steal the car, that was clear.

As realization dawned on him, his expression went from distraught to hurt. "Does Mr. Beaumont think I took his Barracuda?"

"No." I raised a conciliatory palm. "Your name only came up because I asked him if anyone had expressed an interest in the car." I pointed from myself to Brody and back again. "This? This was all me."

His features relaxed. "I hope you find his car."

"Me, too." I gestured back to the driveway. "Now get back over there and show your buddies how the game is played."

His upper lip quirked in a half smile before he turned and trotted back to the makeshift court.

Having eliminated Brody Riddle as a suspect, I drove my police bike over to my mother and stepfather's house. The two had given me and my sister Brie an open invitation to dinner, and we took them up on it one night or two each week. It was nice to see my family and it beat the heck out of having to cook for myself.

My stepdad worked out front, pruning the dead blooms off the camellia bushes he'd planted at my mother's request. He was a pale, doughy man, with thick glasses and zero sense of style. He was also the kindest, most caring, and reliable man I'd ever known. I loved him with all my heart and then some. My biological father? Not so much. The only thing I felt for Sam Sharpe was contempt, especially after seeing his sorry face again last weekend. He'd taken off twenty years ago with the cash my mother had earned as a cashier at a grocery store. She'd hidden the money in her shoes, hoping he wouldn't find it and blow it on whiskey or cigarettes. I'd been just eight years old at the time. My little sister Brie had been seven. As usual, my father had been "between jobs," an imprecise term that meant he'd screwed up and been fired, yet again.

When Mom couldn't make rent, the landlord evicted us from our apartment. My mother's family had disowned her when she got pregnant at seventeen, and her former friends, unfettered and carefree, had fallen away after she'd given birth to me. She'd had no one to turn to, and too little money to rent a truck to move our furniture out of the place. We'd packed our clothing, toys, and what food had remained in the kitchen into our old wood-paneled station wagon.

For three weeks, we'd slept in the car, which my mother parked in the lot of a 24-hour pharmacy every evening. During the day, she drove it to her job at the grocery store. With her savings gone, Mom could no longer afford childcare. She gave me a key so Brie and I could get into the car after school, where we'd wait until her shift was over. Mom parked the station wagon in a shady spot at the far end of the store's lot, where people wouldn't spot us. She gave us strict orders to keep the doors locked and honk the horn if someone bothered us. We were only allowed to unroll the windows one inch, not enough for anyone to fit their hand through and pull up on the locks. She checked on us during her breaks.

One evening, Mom walked me and Brie down the block to play in the park. We'd tired of being cooped up in the car for hours every day. When we returned to the pharmacy, our car—*our home*—was gone. The store manager told Mom the parking lot was for customers only, and that he'd had our car towed.

We took a bus to the outskirts of town, then walked for what seemed like miles until we came to the tow lot where our car had been taken. My mother pleaded with the greasy-haired man in the rusty trailer that served as the lot's office. She didn't have enough money to pay the exorbitant towing fee. I remember the guy dangling Mom's car keys from his fingers, giving my mother a scary smile, and saying *"Maybe there's another way you can pay."* Mom followed him into another room, fear and shame in her eyes as she closed the door behind her. A few minutes later, she'd burst out the door, keys in hand, and hollered for me and my sister to follow her to the car. She'd sped out of the place, tires spinning in the gravel, a cloud of dust in our wake.

She'd driven to a fast-food joint, where she took us to the ladies' room. She'd washed her hands with steaming hot water for ten minutes straight, scrubbing them raw and using all the soap in the dispenser, as if she couldn't get clean. Her fingers were pink and pruny when she finally gave up.

When we left the burger place, she'd driven to the grocery store. She feared she'd lose her job if we were found sleeping in our car there overnight, but she didn't know where else to go. Early the following morning, just as the sun began to peek over the horizon, we were awakened by a *rap-rap-rap* on the driver's window, which my mother had covered with newspaper. She peeked around it to see the store manager, Mr. Yancey. She'd climbed out of the car to speak with him. Brie and I spied on them from behind the newspaper in the back window. We saw Mom cover her face with her hands, her shoulders heaving as she cried. Mr. Yancey frowned in concern. He held up a set of keys, just like the man had done the night before, but Mr. Yancey's accompanying smile was soft and sweet, not scary at all.

Next thing we knew, Brie and I were eating corn flakes at Mr. Yancey's kitchen table and giggling while his cat tried to lap milk from our bowls. Our mother and Mr. Yancey spoke to two police officers in the front yard. Mr. Yancey frowned again at something the officers said, but it was a different kind of frown from earlier, an angry and frustrated frown. My mother burst into tears again, and the police left.

Our stay at Mr. Yancey's was supposed to be temporary, only until Mom got back on her feet. My sister and I were enrolled in an after-school program at our campus, no doubt paid for, at least initially, by Mr. Yancey. Mom made dinner for the four of us every night, and Mr. Yancey insisted on helping her with the dishes afterward. My mother tried to keep me and Brie corralled in the guest bedroom so we wouldn't invade Mr. Yancey's space any more than necessary, but he invited us to watch television with him in his living room. He even let us pick the shows we watched. He put up a swing set in his backyard. He bought us bicycles and helmets, and taught us how to ride the bikes, running alongside us as he held us up. Once I'd mastered how to balance and maneuver on the bike, I was unstoppable, racing up and down the street at breakneck speed. Riding my bike made me feel free, as if I by going fast I could outrun our family's problems, leave them in my dust.

Over time, my mother began to laugh more often than she cried, until I could no longer remember when I'd last seen her shed a tear. Mom finally saved enough for us to move out and rent furniture. Except we never did. By then, something had developed between my mother and Mr. Yancey, despite the sixteen-year difference in their ages. My biological father had never officially married my mother, so no divorce was necessary. Mom married Mr. Yancey at the courthouse, with Brie and I serving as witnesses. Six years later, to their delight, Mom got pregnant with my half-brother, Jacob.

My stepfather turned and smiled as I walked up. "Hey there, Shae."

"Hi, Dad." Unlike my biological father, this man had earned the title. I gave him a kiss on his soft, pliable cheek. "How're things going?"

He beamed. "Jake earned straight A's on his report card

again this term."

I feigned a scowl. "Show off." My stepdad didn't fall for the ruse. We both knew how proud I was of my little brother. Brie and I had more street smarts than book smarts. Jake was the opposite. He might know the Pythagorean theorem, but he had zero situational awareness. I'd once had to snatch his wallet back from a pickpocket downtown. Too bad I wasn't wearing the badge at the time or I would've arrested the robber. I was glad Jake's life had been safer and simpler than mine and Brie's, that he'd had the luxury of not having to learn survival skills.

Dad tucked the pruning shears into the bucket he'd been using to collect the spent blooms and removed his gardening gloves, laying them on top. "Let's go see what your mom's cooked up for dinner."

We went inside and ventured into the kitchen, where we found my mother stirring spaghetti sauce at the stove. Noodles boiled in another large pot beside it.

"Smells great," I told her as I gave her a peck on the cheek, too. "How can I help?"

"Want to get the garlic bread ready?"

"Sure." I washed my hands and set about slicing the Italian bread and brushing it with olive oil and garlic. After I slid the cookie sheet into the oven to brown the bread, I said, "I'll round up Jake."

I found my baby bro in his bedroom, which looked like it had taken a direct hit from a bomb. Dirty clothing was scattered all about, hanging from the back of his desk chair and doorknobs. Snack wrappers littered the floor and his desktop, along with dirty plates and glasses. His bedcovers and sheets were tangled in a crazy twist atop his mattress. The room bore the funk of garbage and teen-boy testosterone. They don't call it adol*essence* for nothing.

Jake lay back in a specially designed video gaming chair with a headset on, talking trash to his friends over the internet. "You doofus! You just shot me! I'm on your team, idiot!"

Like his father, Jake was pale-skinned, but he'd somehow managed to stay thin despite an utter dislike of physical activity. Credit the high-speed teen-boy metabolism. I stepped up behind him, reached down, and snatched the controller out of his hands, pushing buttons as fast as my fingers could move. Six seconds later, his avatar lay dying, having taken an abundance of laser fire from green-skinned aliens.

"You suck at this game." Jake reached a skinny arm up to grab the controller back out of my hand.

"Nice to see you, too." I ruffled his hair affectionately. Once he'd informed his friends he was going offline, put the device down, and removed his headset, I wrapped him in a tight bear hug. Having immobilized him, I bent him over and ran my knuckles back and forth over his head, giving him the noogie treatment. What were kid brothers for if not to torment?

"Stop that!" he hollered.

When I released him, I held up my hand for a high five. "Way to go on your report card, dude."

He slapped my hand, *hard*, and said, "Dad said if I make straight A's the rest of the year, I can go to summer camp at the Space and Rocket Center in Huntsville, Alabama. How cool is that?"

"*So* cool." Jake would be the first human to set foot on Mars, mark my words. "Dinner's ready. Wash up."

I returned to the kitchen, where my stepfather was setting the table. Brie had arrived while I was rounding up Jake. Brie was a slightly shorter, slightly less busty version of me, with a much better haircut. Her golden hair had been styled into loose curls with fashionably frayed ends. I didn't bother much with my hair most days. There was no point given that I'd end up with helmet head. Brie worked for a local pop radio station, performing a variety of administrative tasks and selling advertising time in between.

Her eyes brightened when I walked in. "Hey, Shae." She stepped over to give me a hug. "What's new with you?"

I wanted to tell her I'd seen our father, arrested him no less, but I didn't want to mention it in front of our mom. I settled for saying, "Not much," which, sadly, was true. My life had become relatively routine. "What about you?"

She grinned. "I got a promotion!"

Mom looked over her shoulder from the sink, where she was draining the pasta. "That's wonderful, hon."

Brie filled in the details. The station manager had finally agreed to put her on the air during the 6:00 AM to 10:00 AM time slot. She'd provide traffic reports every half hour, more often during the morning commute. "I've already decided what my catch phrase will be. 'Roll on, Raleigh-Durham!'"

"That's *wheelie* good," said our stepfather, the grand master of bad dad jokes.

Brie, Jake, and I groaned in unison. Mom, always supportive, giggled girlishly.

Jake pointed a finger at her. "Don't encourage him, Mom."

We took seats around the table, lay our napkins in our laps, and began the process of passing the food around until everyone had filled their plates. We made small talk over dinner, simply enjoying each other's company.

Dad looked at me and Brie. "Either of you know someone looking for work? One of my suppliers is short a loader."

"I'll put the word out," I said. Maybe one of the Dangerous Curves knew someone who needed a job.

"Me, too," said Brie.

While we were on the subject of our jobs, I told them about the classic cars that had been stolen, about Mr. Beaumont and his Barracuda.

"Shoot," Dad said. "Stealing a car from a war veteran is about as low as it gets."

As a cop, I knew things could get much lower, but there was no sense in pointing out this fact and bringing everyone down. "I was right on the thief. Chased him into Chatham County but he got away. Turned off somewhere in the woods."

Jake raised his glass of lemonade. "What do you think the thief is going to do with the car? Use it for parts?"

"Maybe," I said. "But the car is more valuable intact."

"He can't very well drive it, though," Dad said. "If he was spotted in the car, he could get arrested. Maybe whoever stole the car is a collector."

Brie wiped her mouth. "What's the point in keeping a car you can't even drive anywhere?"

Seeing Jake was out of bread, Mom sent the basket his way again. "Without a title, the thief couldn't sell the car to someone else, could he?"

I passed the bread to my brother. "I don't see how. Not in the U.S., anyway."

Durham, North Carolina was a long way from the border. While cars might be stolen in states like California, Arizona, New Mexico, and Texas to be sold south of the border, it would be stupid for someone to nab a car here with the hopes of driving it all the way to Mexico without getting caught. Of course, they could hide the vehicle inside a semi, I supposed.

We wrapped up the meal, exchanged another round of hugs and kisses, and parted on the porch with pleas from my mother to come back again soon. Brie and I headed out to our vehicles. As soon as I heard the front door latch behind us, I said, "Guess who I arrested last weekend?"

She stopped walking and looked up in thought before running through a litany of famous North Carolinians, starting with a local from Chapel Hill. "Clay Aiken?" she asked, referencing the former American Idol contestant on which she'd had a hopeless crush back in the day.

"Nope. I can't really see Clay Aiken in a fight, anyway. He seems like too nice a guy."

"There was a fight, huh? It had to be Sugar Ray Leonard, then."

"Nope."

She cocked her head. "Zach Galifanakis?"

"It's nobody famous."

"Give me a hint, then."

"We share his DNA."

Her head jerked back like she'd been slapped. "I hope you beat him with your nightstick."

"The thought crossed my mind, especially when he said I looked like our 'nagging bitch' of a mother.'"

She shook her head. "I'm glad you didn't tell Mom. It would have only upset her."

"On the bright side," I said, "I've realized the jerk did us all a favor. If not for him walking out, we wouldn't have ended up here." I gestured to the house behind us, where we'd spent many happy years and where our mother was continuing to live happily. Yep, Sunday's ride with the Dangerous Curves had certainly given me perspective. Even so, Trixie was right. I had to work through my remaining feelings about my father if I had any hope of putting my resentment to rest for good.

Brie and I said our final goodbyes, and I climbed onto my bike and motored home.

Back at my apartment, I changed out of my police uniform and into a pair of pajamas. I curled up on the couch with Oscar on my lap and a mystery novel in one hand, a glass of red wine in the other. But as much as I tried to focus on the story, my mind kept going back to the Barracuda. I'd wanted to nab that sucker, and he'd gotten away. *Darn arrogant buck.* He'd cost me an arrest. But come hell or high water, I'd find that car thief and show him just what Shae Sharpe was made of.

Chapter Six

Sticking My Nose Where It Doesn't Belong

The next morning, after roll call, I sat down in one of the shared cubicles and logged into the desktop computer to search for the police reports regarding the classic cars that had been stolen earlier. I printed them out to peruse. All three cars had been stolen from driveways during the late morning hours. Though I'd seen only one person on the security camera footage from the medical center, it seemed likely that more than one person was involved in the crimes. A second person would be needed to drive the car that had brought them to the scene. Then again, I supposed the thief could have taken a cab or Uber to a place nearby and walked the rest of the way. Or maybe he'd left his car nearby and gotten a ride back to it later, after he hid the stolen vehicle.

I checked the reports to see which detective was handling the case. The paperwork indicated that Captain Carter had assigned the car thefts to Detective Richard "Mule" Mulaney. Though the nickname probably originated as a shortened and slightly warped pronunciation of his last name, the moniker was also fitting, as the man was half workhorse, half jackass. He handled the bulk of property crime cases in District Four.

I logged out of the computer and wandered down the hall to Detective Mulaney's office. I stopped in the open doorway and said "Knock knock" to get his attention.

Detective Mulaney looked up from his desk. He was a stocky man, with stiff white hair that stuck up from his head like the bristles of a scrub brush. Ditto for the mustache under his nose. *His poor wife. Kissing him must be like kissing a porcupine.*

The surface of his desk was was crowded yet neat. An abundance of manila file folders lined up in metal holders across the edge of his desk. The names on the file tabs had been crossed through multiple times as each case was solved and the folder repurposed for a new investigation. His stapler and hole punch sat side by side on the corner of the desktop, keeping company with a plastic pencil cup. Given that the guy ran on caffeine, he had his own coffee pot sitting atop his credenza, the half-empty carafe telling me he'd already guzzled several mugs of brew this morning. He must've come in early. As if telling me to hurry up, the wall clock loudly counted off the seconds. *Tick-tick-tick.*

"Officer Sharpe," the Mule said. "To what do I owe this interruption?

"The term is 'pleasure,' sir."

"No, it most definitely is not."

Though he'd yet to invite me into his office, I stepped inside anyway. "I chased the stolen Barracuda yesterday, but lost it in Chatham County. Have you heard anything since from the sheriff's department?"

"Not a word," the Mule said.

I'd fully expected that the sheriff's department would call to say they'd nabbed the car thief, and that Deputy Archer would be featured on the evening news, hailed as the hot rod hero who'd found the missing Barracuda. Part of me was glad the cocky deputy hadn't shown me up, though a larger part of me was disappointed the sheriff's department hadn't found the Beaumonts' car. The couple's happiness was much more important than any accolades.

"I'm curious about the classic car thefts. Do you think the thief plans to keep the stolen cars? It would be hard to unload them without a title, wouldn't it?"

The detective took advantage of my interruption to pour himself a fresh cup of Joe. "There's clever ways to get a government-issued title. Sometimes thieves do what's called 'VIN cloning,' where they use a VIN and title from a similar car that's legit, and pass them off as the VIN and title for the stolen car. Or they could create a fake title. Some people are quite skilled at drafting bogus documentation. Unless a purchaser checks the VIN number on the National Insurance Crime Bureau website to see if the car was reported stolen, they might have no idea they're buying a hot vehicle. Even dealers have purchased stolen cars without realizing it. They aren't required to check the site." He went on to tell me about another fraudulent process called 'title washing.' When a person's car had been rebuilt or totaled by their insurance company, some states issued titles branded as *salvage, flooded,* or *rebuilt* to put others on notice. Some unscrupulous car owners would take their branded title to another state that didn't issue branded documents to get a clean title. "My guess is that whoever stole the cars plans to sell them. Those classic cars can be darn valuable, especially the rare ones."

"What's been done to identify the thieves?"

"I just got the case late yesterday. I interviewed the victims again by phone, asked if they any inkling who might have taken the cars. None did. None of the others had been to the speedway in Charlotte. We got video surveillance from a security camera on the house next door to where the Bel Air was taken. The quality's not good, but we've given it to the media outlets anyway, along with the footage you brought back. You never know. Maybe someone will recognize the guy."

"What are you going to do now?"

He shrugged. "Wait for some evidence to pop up."

"That's all?"

He snorted and swept his open palm to indicate the parade of files spread across his dead. "You see these files, Officer Sharpe? I've got two dozen cases demanding my attention, many with much better leads. I've got to focus my efforts on the crimes I've got a chance of solving."

While I empathized with his situation, I couldn't bear the thought that Mr. Beaumont might never see his car again. "Can I see the footage from the Bel Air theft?"

The Mule growled in annoyance, but pulled the footage up

anyway. The video was dark, taken at nighttime, only the porch light and a streetlight illuminating the field of view. As I watched, a guy in a sweatshirt and jeans jogged past, the hood pulled up on his sweatshirt, obscuring his face. The time stamp indicated it was 2:03 AM. Not exactly the typical time a person went out for run. A minute later, the Bel Air headed past in the opposite direction, the man in the hoodie at the wheel.

I gestured to the screen. "Mind if I talk to that couple? And the other victims, too?"

"Why?" He scoffed. "You think you can investigate this case better than me?"

It was my turn to shrug now. "I don't know. Maybe. We won't know until I try."

He snorted. "No one else would dare talk to me that way. You've got the biggest balls in Division Four, Officer Sharpe."

"You're not allowed to say things like that anymore," I told him. "References to genitalia are frowned upon these days."

Alarm skittered across his face until he saw me wink. While I'd tolerate no sexual harassment or discrimination, a mere crude reference wasn't going to send me rushing to human resources. Besides, I'd considered his comment to be a compliment. While I had no literal balls, I liked to think my metaphorical ones were as big and round as my breasts.

He sat back in his seat, his facial features relaxing in relief. "All right, Sharpe. Tell me why you think I should let you perform another round of interviews."

Although not invited to do so, I took a seat on one of his wing chairs. "Because I want to help these people. I know what it's like to discover your car's been taken from you."

"You had a car stolen?"

"Our family car was towed when I was a kid."

He rolled his eyes. "That's not the same thing at all."

I didn't bother to fill him in, to tell him about the panic we'd felt when not just our car, but our shelter and all of our belongings, had disappeared. "Maybe not. But I also don't like that I was on the thief's tail yesterday and he got away from me."

"Ah, now I get it." A smug smile curled his lips. "You want to even the score, repair your ego."

While the status of my ego was a much lower priority than seeing the Beaumonts reunited with their beloved Barracuda, the Mule's statement bore some truth and I wouldn't deny it. "Sure. If I can."

My honest admission melted his smug smile. "Been there myself. It's frustrating when a bad guy slips through your fingers." He let out a long breath. "I suppose it can't hurt for you to perform second interviews. But clear it with Captain Carter first, make sure she's okay with it."

"Thanks, sir."

I stood and gave him a salute before traipsing down the hall to the captain's lair. Unlike the Mule's office, which was strictly utilitarian and bore no traces of personality, Captain Carter's space was unmistakably hers. Like the woman herself, the space was a unique blend of fierceness and femininity. A half dozen potted ferns graced the desk and bookshelves. The walls had been painted bright red to best complement the artwork that adorned them, vivid prints of paintings by the late artist Gwendolyn Knight, who'd once taught at Black Mountain College in Asheville. Also adorning her walls was a large group photo of her former SWAT unit and the paper target that had helped land her a position on the team. Every shot had been a direct bulls-eye.

Her chair was turned to face the window behind her, and all I could see was the top of her head.

I tapped a knuckle gently on her doorframe. "Captain Carter?"

"Officer Sharpe," she replied, recognizing me by my voice. She spun around in her chair and treated me to a broad smile.

"What's up?"

I pointed down the hall in the direction of the Mule's office. "Detective Mulaney told me to get your permission before I go speak with the people whose cars were stolen."

She arched a brow. "He asked you to help with his case?"

I couldn't blame her for being skeptical. The Mule wasn't exactly known as a team player. "I offered."

"Why?"

"The Barracuda was taken from an elderly couple. The husband is a disabled veteran and he's dealing with some health issues. The car meant a lot to him. I'd like to do what I can to get it back."

Her brow fell back into place, and she looked at me from under it. "You're a beat cop, Officer Sharpe. Investigating isn't really your place, is it?"

Once again, my place in law enforcement was in question, just as Deputy Archer had questioned it when I'd chased the car thief into Chatham County. But, despite jurisdictional issues and job descriptions, weren't we all on the same team at the end of the day? "Maybe it's not my place," I admitted. "But the Mule's got a big caseload and could use some help. Besides, I'd bet a lot of people thought a woman didn't belong on the SWAT team, either." I gestured to the photo on her wall and arched my own brow back at her.

"Touché." Rather than chastising me for my insubordination, she seemed to appreciate my determination. That's what made her a great boss. She didn't need her ass kissed, and she brought out the best in her force. "What the heck, Sharpe," she said. "Show me what you've got. Just don't let it get in the way of your other duties."

"I won't. Thank you, ma'am."

Permissions secured, I returned to the cubicle and phoned the couple who owned the Bel Air, Violet and Harry Wellborn. Luckily, they were home. I hopped on my motorcycle and drove out to their place to speak to them. They lived in a brick townhouse, an end unit with flowering purple rhododendron bushes out front. I rounded up my laptop from my hard-sided saddlebag and carried it to the door with me.

Like the Beaumonts, the Wellborns were a retired couple. They invited me inside, where I was offered a seat on an outdated velveteen sofa and a glass of sweet tea. I took both and, after a sip of tea, launched into my questions. "How long had you owned the car?"

"Not long," Harry said in that non-specific southern way of talking that begged for a follow-up question.

I had to hazard a guess at how long *not long* was. "A month or two?"

Violet clarified for her husband. "Two years and three months. I bought it for Harry for our golden anniversary. His first car was a Bel Air. Harry and I were high school sweethearts, and we went on dates in the car." She nudged her husband in the ribs with her elbow. "We had some fun times in that car at the drive-in, didn't we?" When Harry blushed, Violet laughed and turned her attention back to me. "He got rid of his Bel Air shortly after we were married. It was an old car even then, and had become a money pit. As we were coming up on our anniversary, I was looking through our wedding album and saw photos of us leaving the ceremony in the Bel Air. Our friends had tied tin cans to the back bumper. Made all sorts of racket as we headed off." She smiled, as if the memory brought her joy. "Harry had mentioned the Bel Air now and then through the years, and I thought it would be fun to surprise him with one like it."

"Best surprise I ever got," he said. "Fortunately, this one had a rebuilt engine and ran good."

As I readied my pen to take notes, Violet said she'd found the car online, on a site called VintageVehicles.com. "It was over in Knoxville, Tennessee, but the guy who owned it was willing to drive it here for me to look at."

I jotted down the information. "Detective Mulaney said you

haven't taken the car to any classic car rallies, but has there been anyone who's shown an interest in the car somewhere else?"

"Too many people to count," Harry said. "Someone's always commenting on it when we're at the gas station or getting in or out of it in a parking lot."

"Have you noticed anyone following you home?"

"No," Harry said. "But we haven't been looking, neither."

I twiddled the pen between my fingers. "Has anyone who's admired the car asked where you lived, or asked your names?"

"Hmm," Harry said, looking up at the ceiling as he seemed to be thinking back. "Seems like some guy at a gas pump gave me his name and offered his hand awhile back. Asked me what year model the car was, took a look in the windows to check out the interior."

"Do you remember the man's name?"

"Not at all. Didn't seem important at the time."

"Did you give him your full name?"

"More than likely," he said. "If a fellow gives me his first and last name, it's my habit to give my full name back. My mama taught me that was the polite thing to do."

With a full name, the guy could have tracked Harry Wellborn's address down through the property tax records or landline listings. *Good manners, coming back to bite him in the butt.* "Which gas station were you at?"

"Couldn't tell you to save my life." Harry raised both his shoulders and his palms. "I don't go to any particular one regularly. I just stop at whichever one's around whenever the tank runs low."

"Do you remember what the guy looked like?"

He consulted the ceiling again. "If I recall correctly, he was a white guy with dark hair. What I could see of it anyway. I believe he was wearing some type of hat and sunglasses."

"Any facial hair?"

"Could be he had a beard. Seems all the young men have beards these days."

"Age?" I asked.

"Thirty or so?" he said, unsure.

"Do you remember what kind of car he was driving?"

"Couldn't say. I've got only a hazy memory of talking to the feller."

It was understandable. After only an hour or two, I'd be hard pressed to identify a driver I'd pulled over and cited. Our minds move on and don't retain details that seem inconsequential.

I booted up my laptop, inserted the thumb drive, and showed him the video footage from the medical center. Pointing to the screen, I asked, "Is that the same guy you spoke to?"

"Can't say for sure one way or another," Harry said. "It's been a while and, like I said, I didn't get a good look at the guy."

I thanked Harry and Violet for their time and the tea, returned to my motorcycle, and pulled out my cell phone to call the owner of the Charger. He was at his bartending job in a Mexican restaurant, but said he could speak to me if I came by. Fifteen minutes later, I was sitting on a stool while he worked on the other side of the counter, stocking glasses on the shelves. The guy was mid thirties, Latino, and looked like he worked out in his spare time. I asked him about the car.

"I've always had a thing for muscle cars," he said. "Got it from my grandfather. He was a mechanic, owned a garage here in town. He left me the Charger when he passed away a few years ago. I love the feel of older cars. You're really in control, you know? The cars made these days are so automated they practically drive themselves."

Heck, in some cases, cars actually did drive themselves now. I asked him the same questions I'd asked the Wellborns.

Unfortunately, his responses were similarly vague. People often commented on his car when he stopped for gas. Nobody in particular stood out to him. He didn't recall anyone asking his name.

I'd brought my laptop into the bar and set it up on the counter. "Take a look at this security camera footage." I showed him the video clips from the Bel Air and Barracuda thefts.

As he watched, his eyes narrowed and he rubbed his chin thoughtfully. "This could be nothing, but about a month ago I came out of the restaurant and found a guy bending down next to my car. He told me he'd dropped his phone. I didn't think much about it at the time, but the guy in these videos could be the same guy. He was wearing sunglasses and had a beard."

"Was there anything else distinctive about him?"

"There were blue flecks around the edges of his beard. Looked like glitter. I thought maybe he'd visited that strip club down the block, picked up the glitter during a lap dance."

Glitter might not be the only thing he'd picked up. "Any chance you saw the vehicle he was driving?"

"No. I didn't pay any attention to where he went when he walked off."

It crossed my mind that the guy might not have actually dropped his phone. He might have been placing a magnetic vehicle tracker on the car. The devices cost less than a hundred bucks and allowed a person to track a vehicle's precise location from their computer or cell phone. It also crossed my mind that the guy could have been painting a car, disguising it under a different-colored coat so he could sell it without raising suspicions. While most house paint would be flat in color, metallic paint, such as that used on vehicles, would sparkle like glitter. The final thing that crossed my mind was that it was nearing lunchtime and the Mexican food cooking in the kitchen at the back of the restaurant smelled *muy bueno*. Of course, lunch would be more fun with an *amiga*. I texted Amberlyn, who met me there for chips, salsa, and enchiladas. Being on the clock, we had to forego margaritas.

After lunch, I headed to an office building downtown to speak to the owner of the Aston Martin, an attorney who specialized in wills and estates. Judging from his posh penthouse office, his well-tailored suit, and the Cartier briefcase resting on his credenza, helping people plan for death was a good way to make a living. From his window, I could look down into the Durham Bulls ballpark where the Triple-A baseball team played. The water tower at the American Tobacco campus stood even with his window, the words LUCKY STRIKE on the metal having faded over the years. The tower at Duke University Chapel loomed a mile or so away, the gothic structure reaching up to the sky.

"May I offer you a sparkling water?" he asked.

Who was I to refuse some hoity toity H2O? "That would be great. Thanks."

He retrieved a bottle from a mini fridge cleverly disguised in a cabinet and poured it into a glass for me. I took a sip, the bubbles tickling my nose and causing me to sneeze. *Snit-snit.* Classy, huh?

We took seats at a glass-top table and I showed him the videos. He didn't recognize the thief in either clip, though he did mention a clean-shaven, ginger-haired valet at an upscale restaurant in Raleigh who'd seemed especially interested in the '64 Aston Martin DB5. "He recognized it as the car James Bond drove in several movies. That's precisely why I bought the car. I'm a big Bond fan. At any rate, the valet asked if he could take a selfie behind the wheel."

"Did you let him?" I asked, curious.

"Gladly," the man said. "He'd been polite enough to ask permission, and a car like that is meant to be enjoyed. Of course, someone else is enjoying it now, I suppose."

I figured the valet was unlikely to be the culprit who'd taken the vehicles. None of the other victims had mentioned a valet, or anyone with reddish hair. And anyone intent on taking the car would probably have been more subtle.

We wrapped things up and I returned to the District Four

station to update the Mule.

I plopped myself down in one of his wing chairs and told him what I'd learned in my interviews. When I asked Detective Mulaney if he thought the blue paint flecks could be an important clue, he expressed both interest and a healthy amount of skepticism, the latter developed over years of chasing false leads.

"The paint might mean something," he said, "or it might mean nothing at all. We don't even know if the guy had anything to do with the disappearance of the Charger. You said the bartender wasn't sure the guy he saw by his car is the same one from the videos. That said, if the thief is painting the cars, he'd need a place to do it. A garage or a barn with good ventilation. He'd also need some skill in that regard. Hell, he could've learned in prison. They teach the inmates how to paint vehicles in the auto shop classes. They repaint government vehicles, fire trucks and whatnot." He suggested I search the criminal database and police reports for anyone in the area who had been convicted or accused of car thefts in the last ten years. "Go talk to them, see if you get any suspicious vibes. Let me know what you find out."

"So first you treat me like I'm meddling, and now you actually want my help?"

"Hell, yeah," he said. "You not only have the biggest balls in the division, you've got the biggest heart, too. You give a shit. That's why you work so hard. I might as well put your concern to good use."

Though I was again flattered by his words, I knew my fellow officers cared about their work, too, about the people they served. Those who didn't have an aptitude for public service generally didn't last long in this stressful and often thankless profession.

I left the Mule's office and went down the hall, where I slid into a cubicle to search for any car thieves who might be in the area. But before I checked the criminal records, I decided to take a look at the report for that long-ago visit between my mother, Mr. Yancey, and the two male officers who'd responded. I'd never pulled it up before, tried to pretend it had never happened and move on. But pushing my feelings down hadn't been worked. Trixie said I should confront things head on. Reading the report would be my first step.

Chapter Seven

Better Left Unread

My gut twisted as I read my mother's statement. Though I'd been too young at the time our car had been towed to fully understand what had taken place in that metal building at the tow lot, as I grew older I suspected my mother had been forced to give the creep at the tow yard a "happy ending" in order to get our car back. Her statement confirmed it. She'd told the officers that she'd had insufficient funds to redeem our station wagon, that the man at the tow lot took advantage of her desperation, and that she'd felt she had no other choice but to give the creep the hand job he'd demanded in order to get our car and belongings back. No wonder she'd nearly scrubbed her skin off in the burger joint's bathroom. As noted in their report, the officers on duty saw the situation differently, suggesting my mother had engaged in an act of prostitution by providing sexual gratification to pay the towing fee. Fortunately, things had evolved since that time, and people were generally more sensitive to the nuances of such situations. Even so, it was a damn good thing the two officers had since retired from the department, or I just might have taken my nightstick to their nards.

As I stared at the screen, I caught my reflection, my eyes looking back at me, filled with hurt and anger. Was this the face my father had seen when he'd glanced back at me from the squad car last Friday night? I supposed it was. I decided that, while I was already in the police reports database, I might as well run a search for my father's name, see what kind of trouble Samuel P. Sharpe had gotten himself into over the years. I'd never looked before, neither in the police nor the criminal records. It had seemed easier to pretend the man had never existed, that I'd been conceived in some type of immaculate conception, minus the angels, manger, and gifts from the magi. *What would I have done with frankincense and myrrh anyway?*

I typed my father's name into the search box and hit the enter key. Over a dozen reports came back. I started with the oldest, which was from 1978, when my father would have been only five or six years old. While the names of minors were redacted from public copies of police reports, as an officer I had access to the complete documents. By the time I finished reading the reports, I was shaking and heartbroken and sick.

In the few years he'd spent with us, my biological father had never mentioned his family. After he'd left, I avoided bringing him up, knowing it would only upset my mother. But now I knew more about his family and childhood than I would have ever wanted to, and it was a complete nightmare. The scars on my father's hand weren't from a dog bite, as he'd told us. They were cigarette burns, his mother's boyfriend using her small son as an ash tray for punishment. When she'd refused to break ties with the brute, child protective services had taken my father away and placed him with his maternal grandmother, who'd gone on a bender and forgotten to feed him or send him to school for days on end. A concerned school bus driver had notified the authorities when my father didn't show up at the bus stop for several days in a row. He'd been emaciated when they'd found him. And all of this was just for starters. He'd bounced around among an extended family who'd managed to keep him alive, but had certainly not nurtured him.

When he turned 18, the police reports began to address petty crimes committed by my father rather than against him. A misdemeanor drug offense for possession of a small amount of marijuana. A vandalism charge in which he'd punctured a tire on his boss's car after being fired from a job. A couple of assaults. The most recent report was my own from the preceding weekend. A quick look at the criminal records confirmed he'd never been charged for the assaults. None of the victims appeared to have suffered more than superficial injuries, with my father taking the brunt of the blows. The district attorney must have figured it wasn't worth the time to pursue the matters.

I logged into the database to find out the disposition of my father's recent arrest at the biker bar. I was curious whether he'd yet been arraigned, how he'd pleaded, whether I might have to testify against him at a criminal trial. To my surprise, I discovered he was still in custody. In other words, no one had made bail for him.

I sat back in my seat, fighting down the emotional head gasket that threatened to blow inside me. *Maybe these reports had been better left unread.* But no. I'd looked back, and now I had to move forward. Only I didn't know exactly how.

Bustling in the hall caught my attention and my eyes went to the clock on the wall. It was straight up 5:00 and officers were rotating off the day shift, others rotating on to the swing shift. I decided to wait until the morning to run my search for the car thieves. I pulled out my cell phone and called Trixie. "Can I come by? I need to talk."

"Of course," she said. "I just ordered a pizza. We can share it."

"I'll bring the root beer."

#

Half an hour later, Trixie and I were sitting in rocking chairs on the front porch of her bungalow in east Durham, enjoying hot pizza and cold root beer, her favorite drink.

I told her what I'd found in the records. "No wonder my father was so screwed up." While military men were the poster children for PTSD, the ugly truth was that families who'd battled on the home front also suffered the disorder at alarming rates. No doubt my father had lingering issues stemming from his childhood trauma.

Trixie reached out and gave my hand a supportive squeeze, knowing what I'd learned had upset me. "Does knowing all that stuff about his childhood make it easier to forgive him?"

"It does," I said. "But even though it explains his behavior, it doesn't necessarily excuse it."

"So you don't yet have closure. You're not ready to chuck it in the fuck-it bucket." Trixie could always be counted on for a fresh word of phrase.

"Not quite."

She raised her drink. "Keep working on it. You'll get there."

"I hope so." Turning to another topic, I gave her a rundown of the classic car thefts. "I visited some of the victims today. Nothing they said gave us any new leads."

"You're nothing if not determined," she said. "I bet you'll figure things out."

"I hope so." I found myself wondering how Jerry Beaumont was doing, if his broken heart was holding up. I also found myself wondering where my father was right now.

When the pizza was gone and the remaining root beers stowed in Trixie's fridge for next time, I gave her a hug, headed out to my bike, and climbed aboard. My motorcycle seemed to have a mind of its own and took me directly to the county lockup. I stared at the building for a moment, wondering if I'd lost my freaking mind, before going inside.

I stepped up to the front counter. "How much is bail for Samuel P. Sharpe?"

The fiftyish man working the desk put his keys to his keyboard and consulted his computer before returning his attention to me. "Three grand."

"Thanks."

Bonds typically ran 10% of the bail amount, more if the person arrested had skipped out before. Given that my father's bail had been set relatively low, I assumed he hadn't failed to appear previously. I headed out of the jail and drove to an ATM, where I withdrew three-hundred in cash. I drove back the way I'd come, turning into the parking lot across the street from the jail at the conveniently located bail bondsman's office.

The man at the front desk cocked his head in surprise. "A cop posting bail? That's a first."

He stared at me, as if waiting for a response. I didn't owe this man an explanation, and I wasn't going to give him one. I pulled out my notepad and jotted a quick note that read *Consider this an early Father's Day gift.* I signed my name, and added both my phone number and my e-mail address. I folded the note and picked up a stapler from the desk to staple it closed. I handed the note to the man. "Make sure Mr. Sharpe gets this when he's released."

With that, I went out the door. Would my father get in touch with me? It seemed unlikely. My mother still worked at the same grocery store where she'd worked when they'd been together. He could have easily found her there, yet he'd made no attempt to contact us in the last twenty years. But I'd opened a new door now. It would be up to him to come through it.

#

I heard nothing from my father that night and, the next morning, my attention was back on the car theft investigation. As soon as Captain Carter completed roll call, I plunked myself down at a desk and searched to see who in the area had arrests or convictions for car theft. I disregarded the thefts that were crimes of opportunity, where the victim left the keys in the car. Amazing how many people left their cars running in their driveways to warm them up on cold winter mornings, only to come out a few minutes later and find the car gone. I also disregarded the reports that involved the theft of a single car from a related party, such as a roommate, friend, or family member. They didn't fit the classic car thief's M.O. His thefts were targeted and planned. He'd also had no access to the car keys, having to hot wire the vehicles instead.

Three names popped up as possibilities. The first guy was back in jail, this time on drug charges. The second held no current North Carolina driver's license, and had no vehicle registered here. Presumably, he'd left the state. The third was a thirty-three-year-old man named Devin DelVecchio.

DelVecchio's mug shot was more of an *ugh* shot. The guy was as ugly as they come, with bulbous eyes, bumpy skin, and no distinguishable neck. As if that wasn't bad enough, his olive skin bore a greasy sheen that said he hadn't bathed in a while. He resembled a bullfrog. He'd been arrested six years ago for stealing cars and selling them to chop shops. He'd been convicted and served eighteen months at the Dan River Prison Work Farm, a minimum security facility for nonviolent offenders. I jotted down DelVecchio's address and headed out to pay him a visit.

I rapped on the door of the townhouse where DelVecchio lived. The human bullfrog answered a moment later, a can of cheap soda in one hand, the TV remote in the other. He made a guttural sound when she saw my uniform, not unlike a croak. He wore a dingy, sweat-stained undershirt that rode up on his round belly, exposing his navel and four inches of rolled flesh. He didn't have a beard, though it would have been easy enough to shave it off and change his look. Still, his Homer Simpson physique told me he wasn't the guy in the security camera videos. Just in case he might have partnered with the car thief, I told him why I was there. "I'm looking into some car thefts that happened recently in Durham."

He was matter of fact. "I don't know anything about that. I don't boost cars no more."

"Why not? Did you find Jesus while you were in the pen?"

"Nah. There's not enough money in it."

His pragmatic response gave me little hope that he'd turned himself totally around, but his claim that he wasn't stealing cars seemed truthful. Still, even though he might not be involved in car thefts, he could know someone who was. "What about your former associates? You know anyone who might be involved in stealing classic cars?"

He shook his head. "Car theft is a dying business. Like coal mining and tobacco. Everybody I used to deal with is doing other stuff now."

"Like what?"

His bullfrog chin bounced up and down as he laughed sarcastically. "Like I'm going to tell a cop."

"Eh. It was worth a shot."

Having struck out with DelVecchio, I decided to head back to the station to update the detective. On the drive, I was derailed by dispatch coming over the radio, reporting a downed tree on Highway 54. Fallen trees were a frequent problem in the area. Though most fell during or immediately after severe storms, some came down at random, as if trying to keep people on their toes.

I activated my mic. "Unit M2 responding."

In minutes, I pulled up behind a long line of cars that had backed up in the right lane on the roadway. Many were executing U-turns in the left lane, which was devoid of oncoming traffic. The lack of northbound vehicles told me the tree blocked the road in both directions.

I eased over onto the shoulder and rode along until I came upon both the obstruction and the sign demarcating Durham and Chatham Counties. A sixty-foot red maple growing on the Chatham County side had toppled over and lay across the asphalt, its roots exposed and its upper limbs stretching across the border into Durham County. The northbound traffic on the other side of the tree was likewise U-turning. Fortunately, the tree had come down clean, missing the cars on the road.

I squeezed the button on my radio to contact dispatch. "The tree originates in Chatham County." In other words, even though it was now lying partially in Durham County, it was their problem to rectify.

The dispatcher came back. "I'll get the sheriff's department out there."

A short time afterward, an SUV came rolling up on the shoulder. Deputy Archer sat at the wheel. He eased to a stop a few inches shy of the county line, putting our vehicles nose to nose, and climbed out of the Tahoe. He strode toward me, his gleaming roguish gaze locked on mine. "Well, well, well. If it isn't Officer

Sharpe, pushing the limits once again."

I angled my head to indicate the fallen tree. "Seems you've got problems keeping your wood up in Chatham County."

He returned the jibe in kind, lifting his chin to point to the line of cars behind me. "Shame this tree fell here with so many people trying to escape Durham County for Chatham."

He turned and headed back to his SUV, where he pulled a chainsaw from his cargo bay. After donning canvas gloves and yanking the starter to rev it up, he returned to the road and proceeded to cut limbs from the main trunk of the tree. I headed toward him to help move the limbs out of the way. He turned off the saw and raised a palm. "Stay on your side," he teased. "We don't need you infesting us with those big-city cooties."

I rolled my eyes. Mutual aid agreements between law enforcement agencies stipulated that we could work together, regardless of official jurisdictions, during emergency situations. A downed tree impeding the safe flow of traffic constituted just such an emergency, and we both knew it. "Stop me," I said in challenge. I made a show of crossing the boundary by taking a giant step over the invisible line that divided us.

Cutting me some side eye, he revved the chainsaw back up and continued his work. I grabbed the limbs he'd cut and carried them off the road, stacking them on the shoulder. Once he'd dispatched the limbs, he set to work on the main trunk of the tree, cutting it into logs about two-feet long. Rather than break my back trying to lift them, I put my biker boot to the logs and pushed, rolling them to the edge of the roadway with my feet. Fifteen minutes later, Deputy Archer and I had the roadway cleared, and traffic began to flow freely again.

He slid the chainsaw back into the bay of his SUV and slammed the door closed. Gesturing to the road sign, he said, "Emergency's over now. Git."

"Gladly." I stepped to the sign and stopped, pretending to wipe my feet at the edge of Chatham County before stepping back into Durham. I climbed onto my bike, started my motor, and circled around to his side of the sign before giving him a *beep-beep* of my horn and gunning it to zoom off in style.

As I headed back to the station to speak with the Mule, I passed a car dealership. The brand new vehicles sparkled in the morning sun. Someone must have come in early to wipe off the pine pollen that left a thick yellow-green dusting on vehicles this time each spring. At the front of the lot, a bright red inflatable dancing man bent over and straightened up, flailing his arms like a suspected drunk asked to touch his nose during a sobriety test. Passing the dealership gave me an idea . . .

Fifteen minutes later, as I stepped into his doorway, the Mule looked up from his desk. "Any luck solving my case?"

"Not yet."

He slugged back a mouthful of coffee and leaned back in his seat. "Detective work's not as easy as it looks, is it?"

"Not at all." I thought I'd gather up clues like puzzle pieces, put them together, and get a clear picture of the crime. But, so far, nothing had panned out. After informing him that I'd struck out visiting DelVecchio, I said, "What if I pay a visit to the classic car lots in town? Maybe one of them is involved or has been approached by someone trying to sell the cars or their parts."

"Can't hurt," he agreed. He fished a stack of business cards out of his desk and handed them to me. "Ask them to call me if they learn something."

I headed out again to make the rounds of the garages and auto lots that dealt in classic cars and parts. My first visit was to Masterpiece Motors. All of the vehicles for sale were parked inside an enclosed showroom, and had been impeccably detailed. I'd never seen such immaculate paint and clean tires. The place offered only a few select cars, including a 1957 Ford Thunderbird convertible with some type of limited edition supercharged engine. The sticker price was over $200,000. *Sheesh! You could buy a house for that chunk of change.*

The owner came out of his office and greeted me with a

smile. He wore khaki pants and a navy blue blazer along with a white button down shirt, the typical prep school uniform. "Good day, Officer. Something I can help you with?"

"Are you aware of the classic car thefts that have taken place in Durham and Raleigh?"

"Sure am. Saw the report on the evening news. I didn't recognize the guy in the video footage, but I'm keeping an eye out for him. If he tries to hit my lot, he'll be sorry." He patted his hip, letting me know he had a handgun at the ready. The concealed carry law gave him the right to be armed, but I hoped the car thefts wouldn't lead to violence and bloodshed. No property was worth more than a human life.

"We're not sure if the thief is a collector, or if he's stripping the cars for parts or disguising them with new paint and other cosmetic changes to resell them." I handed him the Mule's business card. "If anyone offers to sell you the same model as the missing cars, or parts for the cars, please get their contact information and give Detective Mulaney a call. Don't let the seller know you're on to him, okay?"

"Will do."

My next stop was at Rare Auto Repair, a garage that specialized in fixing unique vehicles, including older and imported models. A curvy red classic convertible Corvette was parked alongside the building. *Sweet ride.* I glanced into the open bays as I approached the office. An eighties-era black Trans Am was up on one lift, while an ancient white Ford Fairlane sat in the other bay, its hood open as if a doctor had asked it to say "ahhh." Three mechanics in grease-stained coveralls moved about the space, tools in hand.

The gray-haired woman working the front was also familiar with the thefts. "One of our clients said something about it, so I read up on the situation on the internet. Any luck finding the cars?"

"Not yet," I said. "I'm hoping I can count on you to help us out."

"Anything I can do," the woman said, "I'd be glad to."

"You can keep an eye out for the cars, let Durham PD know if anyone contacts you about similar cars or their parts. Sound good?"

"Happy to help," she said, taking the detective's card.

I jerked my head to indicate the bays. "Mind if I speak with your mechanics?"

"Have at it," she said.

I stepped into the garage area. "Excuse me," I called to the men. When all three sets of eyes were on me, I asked if they'd been approached by anyone about an Aston Martin, Charger, or Barracuda.

"You mean the ones that were stolen?" asked one of the men.

"Exactly," I said. "We're thinking the thief might try to move them through the classic car circles, or maybe try to sell the parts."

All three indicated that they'd heard nothing yet.

"If you hear anything," I said, "even rumors, please get in touch. Those cars meant a lot to the people they were taken from."

"I can imagine," said one of the guys. "My '78 Corvette is my baby."

Good to know they're on our side. I thanked them and left.

While I knew many body shops had the equipment and facilities to paint the cars, there was no way I could visit every auto shop in town. I hit the MAACO facility, however, and asked them whether anyone had brought in a car fitting the makes and models of the stolen classics.

"No," the manager said. "I'd remember if anyone had brought in an unusual car like any of those."

Having put out what feelers I could and exhausting the leads within the jurisdiction of Durham PD, I set out on patrol feeling frustrated and defeated. The longer the Beaumonts' car was missing, the less likely we were to find it. The other cars, too. *Argh!*

#

Over the rest of the workweek, I repeatedly ran searches online for cars being offered for sale. I ran across a 1971 'Cuda for sale in Winston-Salem. Even though it was purportedly a year newer than Jerry Beaumont's car, I nevertheless rode the hour and a half out there to check it out. While my research indicated the early Barracuda bodies were based on another model, the Plymouth Valiant, this practice ceased with the 1970 models. The body style between the '70 and '71 models was similar, and the seller might have fudged on the year to keep from being found out.

The paint was bright banana yellow, with a black racing stripe down the side, and the paint job didn't look new. In fact, the paint was chipped in a several spots. My critical inspection of the chips, as well as the doors and wheel wells, turned up no trace of green paint underneath the yellow coating. What's more, while the stolen Barracuda had a reupholstered interior, the interior of this car was a bit shabby, with a few strips of black electrical tape affixed over gashes in the vinyl in a shoddy attempt to conceal them. I even checked the glove box. No sign of a lime-green tire gauge. It was clear the car wasn't Mr. Beaumont's.

"Thanks," I told the man offering the car for sale. "It's a nice ride, but I've just started looking. I want to see what else is out there."

He patted the hood. "You won't find another like her," he warned. "I've had lots of interest. She'll go fast."

I smiled at his unintended double entendre. "I'm sure she will."

I continued my online search. Though I found a few other vehicles that matched the make and model of the stolen cars, they, too, checked out as legit. By Friday evening, I was feeling beyond discouraged at my fruitless investigation. I was also understanding why the Mule had gone with his wait-and-see approach. All my efforts seem to have been for naught, an unnecessary expense of time and energy.

But while my search might have been fruitless, my Friday evening wasn't. The fruit involved was grapes, fermented into a delicious drink that could ease frustrations, at least for a little while. Amberlyn and I commiserated over cheap cabernet in a downtown Durham wine bar.

She slugged back a gulp. "My week was a waste, too. A speeder I clocked doing ninety-seven on Apex Highway a while back challenged the ticket in court. I planned to testify against him, but I got hung up at a fender bender and didn't make it to the courthouse on time. The judge dismissed the citation." She issued a loud sigh. "Sometimes I wonder why we bother."

I thought about Jerry Beaumont, about what little time he might have left, how that empty space in his garage equated to an empty space in his heart. *That's why we bother.*

"On a bright note," Amberlyn added, "I've got a date tomorrow night."

"Oh, yeah?" I said. "With who?"

"Remember that guy I met when we went to the Hurricanes game?"

"How could I forget?" He'd been sitting next to us in the hockey arena. An amateur player himself, he'd taken a puck to the nose in practice. "His nose looked like an eggplant." Not only had it been huge and misshapen, it had also been purple.

"Look at him now," she replied, holding up her phone.

On the screen was an attractive white guy with the same shaggy blond hair, but with a nose only a third the size it had been the night of the game between the Carolina Hurricanes and Vancouver Canucks. His skin bore a slightly yellow tint, but his nose was straight. Overall, he'd healed up nicely.

"Not bad," I agreed. "He got a friend for me?" It had been a while since I'd been on a date. I'd tried nearly every dating app, engaged in hours of online flirtation but, when the guys learned that I was in law enforcement, they either felt too emasculated to take things further or hoped I'd be into kinky play with my handcuffs. *Ugh.* The only guy I'd met in the wild recently was Deputy Archer and, despite the initial jolt I'd felt on seeing his sexy brown eyes, he seemed more like a rival than a romantic prospect.

Amberlyn sipped her wine. "If we have a good time tomorrow night, I'll suggest a double date for next time."

"Great."

She raised her glass and signaled the server for another drink before turning back to me. "I heard Patton got in trouble for humping a suspect."

"Is Patton the new K-9? Or is that the name of his handler with the big ears and hairy arms? I have trouble telling them apart."

"You and me both."

We chatted for another hour, catching each other up on the latest gossip. Once we'd run out of wine and rumors, we called it a night, parting in the parking lot. I went home to Oscar and a lot of unresolved emotions. About the investigation. About my father. And about that damn deputy with the sexy brown eyes. All were equally infuriating.

Chapter Eight

Crossing the Line

When I woke late Saturday morning, I decided to do what I could to resolve those still unresolved emotions, at least the ones about the investigation. The victims and videos had given me nothing to go on, and the visits to the auto dealers and shops had likewise yielded no leads. The only thing I knew for certain was that the Barracuda had vanished in Chatham County. That meant one of two things—either the thief had taken the car to a specific, predetermined location in the county, such as his home or place of business, or the thief had abandoned the car in the county so as not to be caught red-handed.

After a cup of coffee and a quick shower, I threw on a fitted long-sleeved T-shirt, jeans, and my studded biker boots. I pulled my hair back into a ponytail and swiped on some eye makeup. I didn't bother with foundation or lipstick. They'd only guck up my helmet. I rounded up my compact, high-powered binoculars from my police bike, and clipped them to my belt.

After kissing Oscar on the head and admonishing him to be a good boy, I donned my cat-head helmet, eased my Harley out the door, and took off for Chatham County. There was only a mile or so of roadway on which the Barracuda could have turned off between the last time I'd had eyes on him and when I'd met up with the buck and Deputy Archer. With the sheriff's office on alert, it seemed someone would have spotted the car if it had since continued through the county, at least if the thief had used any major roads. There was a decent chance the car was still around the area somewhere, that the thief had abandoned the vehicle somewhere in the woods south of the city. Maybe the car was just sitting there, waiting to be discovered and returned to its rightful owners. I might not be able to solve the crime and nab the thief, but I'd consider it a victory if I could find the Barracuda and put Jerry Beaumont back behind the wheel of his beloved automobile.

I headed south and, ten minutes later, passed the sign telling me I was now in Chatham County. I felt a little tingle, knowing I was back on Deputy Archer's turf. Then again, maybe that tingle was simply telling me my motor needed a tune-up.

I turned down the first possible road the car thief could have taken, and slowed to scan my surroundings. The woods were thick and shady, not easy to see into. A single-wide blue and white trailer sat back among the trees, a children's swing set in the front yard. The only car in the gravel drive was some type of silver sedan. The next house I came upon was a gray Colonial set even farther back from the street, visible only in narrow vertical slices between the tall oaks. The house had a two-car garage, but both garage doors were closed. There was no way to tell if the Barracuda was inside. I pulled over on to the shoulder and raised my binoculars to my eyes, scanning the woods. No Barracuda was in sight, nor was there any outbuilding big enough to house the car.

Though I passed two more driveways, one gravel and one paved in asphalt, whatever houses lay at the ends of them were too far back to see from the main road. A yellow sign warned DEAD END, and I slowed to a crawl, banking to turn back the way I'd come.

The second road I turned down was wider, with a yellow line down the middle. Several smaller roads cut off from it, exponentially expanding the escape routes the thief might have taken. *Ugh.* Clusters of houses on half-acre lots were scattered along the first road, a rural neighborhood. While many of the homes had garages in which the stolen car could be hidden, logic told me a car thief would be unlikely to drive the car into a neighborhood where there would be so many potential witnesses.

I returned to the primary road and turned south again. I'd made it only a little way before a Tahoe came from the other direction, heading toward me. The light bar on top told me the SUV belong to the Chatham County Sheriff's Department, the attractive face on the man in the driver's seat told me Deputy Archer was on duty again today, and the fresh tingle in my tummy told me I might not be as annoyed to see him as I should be. As we passed each other, I felt more than saw him do a double take. The red brake lights reflected in my motorcycle's mirrors indicated he was slowing down behind me. *Was he turning to come after me?* The thought both irritated and excited me.

A minute later, he pulled up behind me, his lights flashing.

Busted.

I eased over to the side, cut my motor, and remained on my bike, waiting for him. His door slammed behind me, his boots crunching on the gravel as he walked up beside my bike. I felt that Taser-like buzz again as he turned to face me. He motioned with his index finger for me to lift my face plate. I flipped it up and stared pointedly at him.

"Officer Sharpe," he said. "I thought that might be you on this bike."

My blond hair and big bust must have given me away.

His eyes narrowed slightly. "What're you doing back in my jurisdiction?"

"Just going for a joyride." I shrugged with feigned nonchalance. "It's a free country."

He eyed the binoculars strapped to my belt. "What are the field glasses for?"

"Bird watching." I beamed at the quick excuse my mind had produced.

"Oh, yeah?" He arched an inquisitive brow. "Seen any

interesting birds today?"

"I spotted a scissor-tailed ruby-throated warbling woodpecker. They're very rare." Also entirely made-up, which was probably obvious. Other than what I'd learned from Toucan Sam, Big Bird, and Woody Woodpecker, I knew nothing about birds and birding.

His brow fell back into place as he issued a soft snort. "I call bullshit on the bird-watching. You're out here trying to figure out where that Barracuda went to."

I crossed my arms over my ample chest. "What if I am?"

"Then you should ride with me."

"Why? So you can claim credit if I find the car? Steal my thunder?"

He shook his head. "You're as hard-headed as your helmet, aren't you, Officer Sharpe?"

"That's what my superiors at the station tell me."

A grin tugged at his lips, which looked incredibly soft and damn kissable.

"Why should I ride with you?" I asked.

"Because you'd have an easier time scouting for the stolen car from my passenger seat. I've logged half a million miles on the streets and highways of Chatham County. I can make sure you don't miss any of the back roads." He jerked his head toward his SUV in invitation.

He had a point. He knew this area far better than I did, and could cover it much more efficiently and methodically. What's more, I could keep a better eye out for the Barracuda if I wasn't also having to watch for traffic, squirrels, and deer. Another plus was that he'd have authority to make an arrest if we happened upon the car thief. I was here only as a civilian today, with no power to make an arrest.

"All right," I said. "I'll ride with you. But I need somewhere safe to park my bike."

"I know just the place," he said. "Follow me."

He returned to his SUV and I followed him to a main artery called Farrington Mill Road. A few miles down, he turned into the parking lot of a small diner with red and white gingham curtains in the windows and wooden planters filled with purple petunias flanking the double glass entry doors. The roadside marquee out front read PAULINE'S PLACE – BREAKFAST SERVD ALL DAY. Looked like they'd been short one letter E and decided to just go with it. The botched spelling might not be good enough for Pat Sajak, but it was good enough for Pauline, whoever she was. I pulled my bike into a space at the far end of the lot. Deputy Archer pulled his SUV into the spot next to me.

He unrolled his window as I removed my helmet and clipped it to my bike. "You had lunch yet?"

Heck, I hadn't even had breakfast. Just the cup of coffee. "No."

"Let's fuel up before we head out." He rolled up his window, opened his door and slid out of the Tahoe.

We went inside. The air was filled with the smells of food frying on the grill and coffee percolating in the pot, along with the sounds of silverware clinking and the murmur of casual conversation. The grill let off a loud sizzle as the cook used a metal spatula to flip hash browns. A glass case filled with assorted fruit pies stood next to the register to our right. A sign on a stand read PLEASE SEAT YOURSELF. Deputy Archer held out a hand to indicate a booth in the front corner.

I slid into one side of the booth and he took a seat in the other. Laminated menus were already on the table, standing upright between a shiny metal napkin dispenser and glass bottles of ketchup and mustard. He held out a menu to me but didn't bother to take one for himself.

"I'm guessing you've eaten here before?" I asked as I

reached for the menu.

"Only two or three thousand times. You can't go wrong with anything on the menu. It's all good."

I took hold of the menu, but he refused to release the other end, forcing me to engage in a brief game of tug-of-war with him. "Are you always this difficult?"

"No." He grinned. "I'm usually much worse."

A tall, dark-haired woman sauntered up and placed a large plastic tumbler of tea in front of Deputy Archer. He gave her a smile in return. Though she turned to look at me, it was clear she was addressing him. "Who's this you brought with you, Zane?"

Zane. Now I knew Deputy Archer's first name.

"Officer Sharpe," he told the woman. "She's with the Durham Police Department."

"Ah," she said, nodding. "I didn't realize this was a business lunch. I thought I'd sensed some chemistry between you two, but I must've been mistaken."

She looked from me to him and back again, as if gauging our reactions. I tried to maintain a poker face, but I feared the warm flush that had raced to my face was obvious.

She tucked her pen behind her ear and stretched out a hand. "Welcome, Officer Sharpe. I'm Pauline." After we shook hands, she retrieved the pencil and readied her order pad. "What can I get you to drink?"

"Dr. Pepper, please." Ironically, while I was sitting here trying to deny any chemistry with Zane, I'd ordered a drink that had been created by a pharmacist, an expert in chemistry.

"You got it." Pauline headed off to round up my soda.

Zane flicked a sugar packet to loosen the granules inside before tearing it open and dumping it into his tea. "You know my first name now," he said as he stirred the tea. "I might as well know yours."

"It's Shae."

"Shae," he repeated, leaning back against the booth and draping an arm along the top of the seat. "Shae Sharpe. Shae Sharpe sells seashells by the seashore."

I rolled my eyes. "Shae Sharpe does no such thing."

"What then, does Shae Sharpe do?" He cocked his head in question.

"Besides hunting down stolen cars?"

"Yeah."

"She rides with the Dangerous Curves motorcycle club, plays Fortnite with her kid brother, and serves as a scullery maid for a spoiled cat named Oscar."

"Dangerous Curves," he mused. "Sounds like a tough bunch."

"We hold our own."

"You good at Fortnite?"

"Not really," I said. "I was never into video games as a kid. I liked to play outside, ride my bike and climb trees. But it's about the only way I can get any time with my brother."

"You're close to your family?"

"Sure am." All but my biological father, who, despite what I'd learned about his traumatic childhood, remained on my shit list. I'd bailed the guy out of jail, provided him with my contact information, and he couldn't be bothered to get in touch with a simple *thank you*? As much as I hated to admit it, it felt like fresh rejection and it hurt. Not as bad as when he'd taken off two decades ago, but still. "What about you?" I asked. "Are you close to your family?"

"Closer than you might suspect."

I wasn't sure what to make of that, but it became a moot point when the waitress returned with my soda and readied her pad. "What'll you have, hon?"

I went for the soup and salad.

She shifted her focus to Zane. "Your usual burger and fries?"

"Make it a double today."

"I will not," she snapped. "You don't need all that beef weighing you down when you might have to chase a bad guy. And you're getting a side salad, too. You need some vegetables."

The exchange told me that Zane must eat here regularly.

He looked up at the woman. "Can I still have the blueberry pie for dessert?"

"Of course you can, sweetie. I'm not a monster." She patted his shoulder before leaving our table again.

"Your turn," I told Zane. "What do you do for fun?"

"Paddle," he said. "I take my kayak out every chance I get."

"You go down rapids and over waterfalls, stuff like that?"

"Hell, no. I prefer flat water. I don't have a death wish, and I don't kayak for the thrills. I do it for the peace and quiet. Being out on the water alone is a great stress reliever."

I could relate. There was something about spending time in nature that restored a person's soul. "When I need to clear my mind, I take my bike out on country roads and putter around for a few hours."

"Sounds like fun."

We chatted while we waited for our food. He mentioned that his favorite places to kayak included the paddle trails at the Alligator River National Wildlife Refuge in the northeastern part of the state, as well as Dismal Swamp State Park which, besides its name, was actually a beautiful place full of ancient cypress trees. The swamp straddled the North Carolina and Virginia borders, and had served as a hiding place for escaped slaves making their way along the underground railroad. I told him about my favorite rides, including the Blue Ridge Parkway in the western mountains and the loop in the southwest arm of the state through area known as the Land of Waterfalls. North Carolina offered no end of natural beauty.

Zane spun the salt shaker between his fingers. "I'm guessing the Durham PD has put some time into trying to identify the car thief. Got any good clues?"

"Only one," I said. "The culprit is a white guy with a full beard. One of the victims thinks he might have seen the guy by his car. He said it looked as if the man had glitter in his beard. My guess is it could have been metallic paint flecks."

Pauline arrived with our plates lined up along her arm and slid them onto the table in front of us.

Zane looked up at her. "Do me a favor. Keep an eye out for a dark-haired white guy with paint flecks in his hair or beard. It might look like glitter at first glance. Call dispatch right away if you see him. He's a person of interest in a current investigation."

"Oooh." She leaned in close, wagged her brows, and whispered. "What did he do?"

Zane whispered back. "I'm not telling you. You can't keep a secret."

She stood up straight and scowled. "I'm rethinking that blueberry pie about now."

"He's not violent," Zane said, "at least as far as we know. But it would really help us out if you'd be on the lookout for him. Inform your crew, too, but tell them to be cool. We don't want word getting out to this guy that we're on to him, whoever he is."

"All right," she acquiesced. "Y'all enjoy your food."

As she left the table, Zane said, "This place serves the best pie in the county. The best biscuits, too. If the guy who took the Barracuda is from around here, he'll show up at the diner sooner or later."

"Good to know." I eyed him pointedly. "Who's 'us?'"

"What do you mean?"

"You told Pauline that if she kept a lookout, it would help 'us' out. You including me now, even though my badge is no good here?"

A mischievous gleam sparkled in his eyes. "Nope. You're just a civilian here as far as I'm concerned. By 'us' I meant the sheriff's department."

I brandished my fork at him. "You're a glory hog. A self-aggrandizer."

He lifted one shoulder. "I've been called worse."

We dug into our meal. While food at rural diners could be dicey, such was not the case here at Pauline's Place. The greens were crisp and fresh and the salad dressing, made in house, rivaled anything I'd tried at far more fancy and pricey restaurants in Durham and Raleigh. The zucchini soup was fabulous, too. When Pauline came to clear our dishes, I gave her an in-person review, "This place should be featured on the Food Network."

Zane put a finger to his lips. "Shh. We don't want all those big-city folks coming out here and forcing us locals to wait in line."

"Speak for yourself," Pauline said to Zane before turning back to me. "You tell anyone and everyone, Officer Sharpe. I'm happy to cook for any comers." She walked away with our dirty dishes, returning a moment later with enormous slabs of blueberry pie.

The pie, too, was delicious, the perfect proportions of pastry and berries. When I finished the last bite I said, "This pie has—"

"A certain *je ne sais quoi*?" Zane suggested, twisting the ends of an invisible mustache.

"*Je ne* say what now?" I replied in my best Cackalacky

accent.

Zane slid out of the booth and stood.

I looked around the table. "Don't we need to wait for our bill?"

"There's only one thing I need to wait for."

The next thing I knew, Pauline had returned to the table and stood on tiptoe to plant her lips on Zane's cheek. *What the—?*

After administering the kiss, she stepped back and straightened his tie. "You be careful out there. Don't go getting yourself hurt or killed."

Zane said, "I won't, Mom."

Mom. Now his *"closer than you might suspect comment"* made total sense.

Pauline turned to me and said, "It was nice to meet you, Officer Sharpe. You be careful out there, too."

"I will. I gotta live so I can come back and have more of that pie."

"It's as good a reason to stay alive as any." She sent me a wink and went on her way.

Chapter Nine

Over the River and Through the Woods

Zane bleeped the locks on his Tahoe and stepped over to open my door for me.

"No need for the chivalry," I said. "This is an investigation, not a date."

"You don't let me get the door for you," he said, "you'll get me killed. My mother taught me to always be a gentleman, and she's watching right now."

I glanced back to see Pauline standing at the glass door, looking our way. "How would she kill you?" I asked as I took his warm hand to lever myself up into the seat.

"She'd smother me in gravy, like a biscuit."

"Eh." I shrugged. "There'd be worse ways to go."

He closed the door, circled around to climb in on the driver's side, and started the engine. We began the afternoon by visiting nearby auto repair shops to look for the man with the paint specks in his beard and to ask them to keep their ears and eyes open for any information about the Barracuda.

At the third shop we visited, we came across a mechanic with light skin, a dark beard, and a similar build to the thief I'd seen in the video clips. There were no paint flecks in his facial hair, but he could have easily washed or combed them out. He had a funny walk though, moving on the balls of his feet with a bouncy gait, like a life-sized marionette. The guy in the video didn't walk that way. I supposed the mannerism could have been faked, but none of the other guys called him out on it, so it seemed they were used to seeing him move in that manner. Though I couldn't be certain, I felt fairly sure he wasn't the guy we were after.

Zane pulled his SUV into the parking lot of a barber shop with the antiquated yet iconic red, white, and blue spinning pole out front. "Let's see if these fellers might know the guy we're looking for."

It was a good idea. Beauticians and barbers crossed paths with a lot of people. Ladies' hair salons were a prime place for local gossip, and men's barbershops were surely the same.

We went inside, greeted by the buzzing sound of electric clippers, the soapy clean scent of shaving cream, and a portly sixtyish man who was not only bald but virtually hairless all over. "Hey, there, Deputy Archer. Need a trim?"

"Not today, sir," Zane said as he stepped up to the counter. He lowered his voice. "Could you round up your guys for a quick discussion?"

The man raised a curious brow, or at least the flesh where a brow would be had he retained any hair. He turned to address the other barbers. "Guys! Come over here a minute."

The men excused themselves and left their clients in their chairs to join us at the counter. Once they were all there, Zane leaned in and spoke softly, "Keep this to yourselves, gentleman, but we're looking for a white guy with a dark beard, might have some paint residue in it. Average build. Might know something about cars. Any of you know someone who meets that description?"

One main raised his shoulders and palms. "I got lots of customers with beards. It's the style now."

I chimed in to clarify. "This guy doesn't keep his beard

nicely trimmed. He leaves it more natural."

"No one immediately comes to mind," said one of them.

"I can't think of nobody, neither," said another.

A third just shook his head.

Zane handed the shop owner his card. "Keep this in your drawer there. Any of you think of somebody, or a guy fitting the description comes in, give me a call right away. Keep it on the down low, though. Don't let him know you're calling in a report. Okay?"

The men murmured in agreement before breaking our huddle and returning to their posts and their waiting clients.

Zane and I went back to his SUV and continued our investigation by driving up and down the county roads, starting in the area where I'd lost the car. Zane confirmed what I'd assumed, that other deputies had responded fairly quickly to his request for assistance when I'd chased the car into the county, and that deputies had covered the primary arteries for the rest of the week. There'd been no further sign of the car. Though it was possible the Barracuda had somehow slipped through the county, Zane agreed that it seemed more likely the car had been hidden or ditched in the area.

I kept my binoculars at hand, instructing Deputy Archer to slow down and pull over on occasion so that I could take a better look at a property. He drove down several driveways so we could examine a place in detail, going so far as to ask one of the homeowners whether we could take a peek into the barn in back of his property. The homeowner had agreed, no questions asked. All we'd found inside was a riding lawnmower, assorted yard tools, and a garden snake who'd slithered inside, seeking a mouse to munch on.

"We appreciate your cooperation," I told the man.

"No problem," he said. "Whatever you're looking for, I hope you find it."

"You and me both, sir."

Down another long, dirt drive, we discovered a car parked in the yard. The car was covered with a blue nylon tarp. I hopped out of the SUV to take a closer look. A quick peek underneath revealed a severely dented Toyota Camry that was missing its windshield, its hood, and three of its tires. Why the thing hadn't been sold for scrap was beyond me. It appeared to be beyond repair.

Zane and I paid particular attention to areas where the woods were especially thick and the car could have been obscured among the fallen trees and foliage. Unfortunately, it was impossible to see more than forty or fifty feet into the dense woods. We didn't dare traipse through them. For one, they were too vast to cover on foot. For another, it would be trespassing. We had no warrant to search private property. What's more, there were ticks, mosquitos, and venomous copperheads to consider.

Various types of gates spanned the entrances to some driveways. Some of the gates were automated and made of ornate ironwork with brick supports on either side. Others were manual gates made of lightweight aluminum and secured by heavy chains and padlocks. While the close-standing trees served as a natural barrier to prevent vehicles from circumventing the gates, some of the property owners had nonetheless added fences around the perimeter of their land, as well as NO TRESPASSING signs. Those were generally people you didn't want to mess with. Meth manufacturers. Gun nuts with enough AK-47's and AR-15's to outfit an army. Purveyors of so-called Southern pride with Confederate flag tattoos and little grasp of basic human hygiene.

The glint of sunshine off metal caught my eye and I made a downward motion with my hand, directing Zane to slow down. "Pull over." I climbed out of the Tahoe and walked to the rail-and-wire fence at one of the properties, raising my binoculars to my eyes. Through the trees, I saw a glimpse of the roof of a large metal pre-fab building, the type many people used for workshops. While the building might be big enough to hide two or three cars in, such buildings weren't unusual out here in this rural area, where zoning laws were more relaxed than in the city. Many who worked in construction trades, landscaping, or even some artistic pursuits erected outbuildings on their property for workspace or storage. The gate and fence might have been installed to secure tools and equipment. Then again, it might have been put up to keep anyone from getting so close they could see what was going on back there. The only way to know was to speak with the property owner.

Zane stepped up beside me, putting his own pair of field glasses to his eyes. "Can't see much from here other than the roof."

I exhaled sharply. "It would be so much easier to run surveillance if we worked in a desert."

"It would also be a thousand degrees and smell like sand instead of the fresh scent of pine."

"Do you always have to be so contrary?"

"I can be agreeable. You just haven't given me much to agree with so far."

"Smart ass." I put my glasses back to my eyes and scanned slowly to the right. The corner of a small one-story wood frame house was visible, along with a foot or so of the front porch farther to the right. What little paint remained on the house was peeling, and the porch railing was giving way to wood rot. "Got any idea who lives here?"

"No," Zane said, "but we can find out."

We returned to the Tahoe. He logged into the laptop computer mounted to his dashboard and ran the address through the driver's license records. I leaned over to get a better look at the screen. *No results.*

"Huh." I sat back in my seat. "Think the place is empty?"

"Could be. Let's see who owns it." He logged into the property tax records and ran the address again. This time, a name popped up. *Elsie Mae Tucker.*

"Let's see what we can learn about Ms. Tucker." Zane ran that name through the DMV records. The woman's most recent driver's license had expired seven years ago. She held only a state-issued ID card now. Not surprising given that her birthdate put her at 94 years old. Zane tapped his index finger on the screen. "This is the address for the Shady Villas Retirement Home over in Siler City."

The place was a city in name only, having a population of around only 8,000. The town's founders must have had big aspirations when they'd named the locale.

Zane went on. "I handled a drug case there recently. A nurse's aide was stealing the residents' prescription pain meds and selling them on the black market."

"That's terrible!"

"Tell me about it. Nobody caught on until a woman reported her mother complaining about the pain from her hip replacement. Turns out the aide had replaced the woman's Percocet with Pepto Bismol tablets."

What an absolutely awful thing to do to another human being. I sat quietly for a moment before asking, "Does it ever get to you?"

"Does what get to me?"

"The awfulness of this job, constantly seeing the worst in people, how horrible they can be to each other."

"Honestly?" he said. "Sometimes it does. But then I have a day like today, and I think maybe this job isn't so bad after all."

"You mean a day when you get a big piece of blueberry pie?"

"The pie's got nothing to do with it." He slid me a sexy sideways smile that told me I had something to do with him enjoying his work today. A blush warmed my cheeks. I turned and looked out my window so he wouldn't notice.

He started his engine. "What say we go talk to Elsie Mae?"

"Let's do it."

Half an hour later, we pulled into the parking lot of the retirement home. It was a stone building shaped like a horseshoe, with administrative offices and a large multipurpose room in the center, a nursing wing to the right, and an assisted living wing to the left. We stopped at the front desk and the receptionist pointed us to a black woman with white hair seated at a square table. She was playing cards with two other ladies and a man.

We stepped up to the table. "Mrs. Tucker?" Zane said. "May we have a word with you?"

The woman looked up at us, her rheumy gaze roaming over us. "You the sheriff?"

"Deputy," Zane said, extending a hand. "Name's Zane Archer."

After they shook hands, I introduced myself, too, and offered a hand.

Mrs. Tucker turned to her friends. "Excuse me a minute." She lay her cards down and pointed an accusing finger at the others. "Nobody look at my cards while I'm gone."

We ventured into the hall, where Zane gave her a quick rundown. "We're here about your place on Whippoorwill Lane."

"Nice place, isn't it?"

"Sure is," he agreed.

"My husband and I raised our family there. The house is a bit rundown now, but the land's worth a small fortune. I'm hanging on to it so I can pass it down to my kids."

Zane said, "We noticed you've got a large metal building out there."

"Mm-hm," Elsie Mae said. "That's where my husband—God rest his soul— stored his fishing boat. That boat was his baby. Not that he ever had much luck on the lake. Most days he'd come home empty-handed." Her eyes narrowed. "Why are you asking?"

"We're trying to locate some property that disappeared in the area."

"Disappeared?" She frowned. "You mean it was stolen?"

"Yes," Zane said.

"What makes you think the stolen property's in the boathouse?"

"Nothing in particular," Zane said, "other than the fact that your place is close to where the property was last seen and the structure would be large enough to contain it. At this point, we're just trying to rule out some of the possibilities, narrow down our search. We're wondering if someone's living at the property."

"Sure, we've got a tenant," she said. "Don't know his name, though. My son handles all of that stuff for me."

"How long's the tenant lived there?" Zane asked.

"Six months or so," she said.

Zane and I exchanged a glance. Six months was more than enough time for the tenant to make a trip down to the DMV to update his driver's license, and three times as long as the sixty-day grace period allowed under state law. Whoever was living there didn't seem to want to go on official record at that address.

I whipped a notepad and pen from my fanny pack. "How can we get in touch with your son?"

Elsie Mae rattled off her son's name and phone number without a hint of hesitation. Her mental faculties remained amazingly acute for someone her age. Heck, I had a hard time remembering my own phone number sometimes, and I was nearly sixty years younger than her.

"You might have a hard time reaching him," she warned. "He and his wife are on a cruise along the French Riviera for their fiftieth wedding anniversary. Reception could be spotty if they're at sea."

We thanked the woman for her time and returned to the Tahoe, where Zane placed a call to the woman's son. The call went immediately to voicemail. Zane left a message, asking the man to give him a call, *"S'il vous plait."* He ended with *"Au revoir."* He slid his phone back into his pocket. "What do you know? I'd thought those two years of French in high school had been a waste of time, but I've used it twice today."

"Ooh la la."

We headed back on Highway 64. As a blue Chevy sedan came rocketing toward us, Zane's gaze shifted to his dash-mounted radar. The LED readout showed 89. The driver must have spotted the light bar on top of the SUV, because he hit his brakes. The car dipped forward for an instant before leveling out and continuing toward us at the speed limit. The fiftyish man at the wheel stared straight ahead as he passed us, another dead giveaway. *Speeding? Who, me?*

"Busted," Zane said.

Zane slowed, flipped on his lights, and said, "Hang on!" as he whipped his SUV around on the shoulder to go after the car.

Hanging on to the handle mounted over the door, I said, "What excuse do you think he'll give you? Full bladder? Family emergency? Broken radar? Late for a funeral?"

He cut me a glance. "Want to make it interesting?"

"Sure. I'll put five bucks on family emergency." As the SUV leveled out, I pulled a five-dollar bill from the pouch on my belt and lay it on his dash.

"My money's on full bladder."

The driver pulled his car over to the side of the road, and Zane pulled up behind him. After matching my $5 bet, he slid out of the SUV, citation pad in hand. He and Zane exchanged a few words, Zane wrote him up a ticket, and the guy was on his way once again.

When Zane climbed back into the SUV, I said, "Well?"

"His wife called and said the backyard chickens escaped their coop. He's on his way home to help her round them up."

"Chickens are family, too." I grabbed the money from the dash and held it up in triumph before stuffing it into my pouch.

Zane glanced at the clock. "My shift's up in half an hour. Maybe you should stick around this evening. I could introduce you to the Chatham County nightlife."

"Can't," I said.

"Got a date with your boyfriend?"

"No."

His brows rose. "Girlfriend?"

"No. Got a swing shift to work."

"So no date, then."

"No."

"What about the boyfriend or girlfriend?"

"Don't have one of those, either."

"But if you were to have one or the other, it would be...?" He cocked his head in question.

"It would be a boyfriend. A rich one with a Ferrari and a mansion. He'd look like Joe Manganiello, too, and he'd treat me like a queen, do all the cooking and cleaning while I sunbathed by the swimming pool."

He cut me some sexy side eye. "Good to know."

Flirting on the job was extremely unprofessional of both of us. But it was a heck of a lot of fun, too.

We drove back to the diner and climbed out of the SUV. Zane walked me over to my bike.

"You busy tomorrow?" he asked.

"No." My pulse accelerated. If the organ were a car, its tires would be squealing. *Is Zane going to ask me on a date?*

"When Mrs. Tucker mentioned her husband having a boat, it got me thinking. I'm fairly certain that property backs up to Jordan Lake. We could take my kayak out tomorrow, find out if we might be able to see anything from the backside of the property."

So not a date. *Dang.* Still, it would be a chance both to see him again and to try to catch the car thief or at least eliminate potential suspects. "Not a bad idea. But if we're going to work this case together, we need to make it official. Have your sheriff contact my captain and request my assistance under our departments' mutual aid agreement."

"You women." He scoffed. "Always wanting to put a label on relationships."

Though I knew he was only trying to push my buttons, I said, "You're the one always telling me I'm out of my jurisdiction here. I'm only trying to dot my I's and cross my T's."

"I suppose that beats dotting your T's and crossing your eyes." He did just that, rolling his eyes inward to look at his nose and earning himself a well-deserved groan from me. He pulled a business card and pen from his pocket and jotted down his phone number and home address. "Come over around noon. That'll give you time to catch some shuteye after your shift, but leave us with plenty of daylight hours to explore that part of the lake."

"Works for me," I said. "See you then."

He stepped back but stood watching as I slid my helmet on and climbed onto my bike. I started the motor and gave the engine a little rev. As I drove off, he watched me go. In my rearview mirror, I watched him watch me. Nearly collided with the marquee sign, too. *How embarrassing!*

Chapter Ten

Taking a Load Off

I was four hours into my swing shift and stretching my legs at Southpoint Mall when my phone vibrated with an incoming text. I pulled the phone from my pocket and read the screen. All it said was *Thanks*. I didn't recognize the number, and no name popped up. Whoever had sent it wasn't in my contacts. *Hmm.*

I typed back. *Who sent this?*

A moment later, a reply came in. *Your father.*

My fingers seemed to type of their own accord. *Working swing. Time for my dinner break. Meet me at Chili's on Fayetteville Road?*

Had I really just asked my father to have dinner with me? It was a risky proposition. Things could go really bad. But maybe Trixie was right. Maybe I needed to work through my feelings and maybe, good or bad, confronting my father is what it would take. Then again, maybe I had lost my ever-loving mind.

Three full minutes passed before his response came in. *Ok.*

I returned to my bike, rode it the block or two to the restaurant, and requested a booth where I could see the door. Twenty minutes passed and I wondered if he'd changed his mind, when the door opened and there he was. I raised a hand to get his attention, and he walked over, his steps short and hesitant. He slid quietly into the other side of the booth. A scab had formed over the split lip he'd suffered last weekend, and his cheekbone still bore a faint bruise. But his clear eyes told me he was sober tonight, and his hangdog expression told me he just might feel bad about the way he'd talked to me the preceding weekend, for blaming my mother for his failings.

I simply stared at him for a long moment. He cast furtive glances at me between toying with the menu and salt shaker.

Finally, I said, "You're welcome."

His gaze met mine and held. Speaking softly, he said, "I didn't deserve that bail money."

I thought back to the police reports from his childhood. "You've gotten a lot of things you didn't deserve."

"I know!" he snapped sitting bolt upright, his posture and demeanor changing in an instant. "I didn't deserve your mother, and I didn't deserve you girls. That's why I left." He looked away, and I could see a vein in his neck pulsing.

"No." I reached across the table and grabbed his wrist, taking it in mine. "That's not what I meant."

He turned to look at me again, and I eased back on my grip. "I meant you didn't deserve this. These scars." I raised his hand before gently releasing it. "You weren't bitten by a dog."

He looked down at the scars then up at me, before turning away again. "How do you know?"

"Police reports."

I sat back and mulled over what he'd just said, about not deserving my mother, my sister, and me. Clearly, his upbringing had left him with no sense of self worth. And though he had been a little older than my mother when they'd met, he'd been hardly more than a kid himself. He'd probably been overwhelmed by the responsibilities of fatherhood, by the end of a childhood he'd never even had a chance to experience. He'd acted immaturely and irresponsibly, but it was understandable under the circumstances, even if wrong.

We shared another long moment of silence before he looked at me again. "I really screwed things up, didn't I?"

"Yes," I said. "But you might be able to unscrew them."

His eyes flashed in surprise and remained bright with hope. "Really? You think so?"

"I wouldn't be here if I didn't. It might not be a total unscrewing, and it might take a while, but I know Mom and Brie. If you explained and apologized, they'd hear you out." I leaned forward. "None of us wants to keep holding on to this resentment. It's been weighing us down far too long, and we've been looking for a reason to let it go. Give us one." He'd probably feel better, too, if we cleared the air. He'd likely been hanging on to a lot of guilt and regret. "Just let me lay some groundwork first. You broke my mother's heart. She might need to ease herself into the idea."

His exhaled a long breath and sat back in the booth, scratching his head in a vain attempt to hide the fact that he'd just wiped a tear from his eye. His voice cracked when he spoke again. "How is she?"

"Mom? She's good. Married. Has another kid, a boy, smart as a whip. Still works part-time at the same grocery store."

He nodded, chewing his lip. "Her husband, is he good to her?"

"The best. He helped us out when you left, took us in."

He nodded again, closing his eyes for a brief moment. "And Brie?"

"Tune into WRNR," I said. "She does the morning traffic reports."

"No shit?"

"No shit."

"Well, I'll be damned." He beamed with pride before looking away again. "I'm glad you two turned out all right." Though he didn't follow his statement with *despite me leaving you in the lurch,* it was clear that was what he meant.

"So what are you doing these days?" I asked. "Besides picking fights at bars."

"Looking for a job. I worked the last six years for a local moving company down in Tallahassee, but they sold out to a bigger outfit and put all the loaders out of work."

"Six years, huh? So you were showing up on time? Doing a decent job?"

"I was. Staying out of trouble, too."

Looked like I wasn't the only one who'd grown up since he'd left.

He grimaced. "But when I came back here, everything just . . ." He shook his head and let the sentence remain unfinished. I could finish it for him, though. Coming back here had brought up a lot of bad stuff, and he'd fallen back into old, destructive habits.

"My stepfather said one of his suppliers is looking for a loader," I said. "You've got experience handling boxes. He might give you a shot. But you'd have to pull your weight."

Dad sat up straight. "I would." The hopeful expression on his face said *especially now that I'd have a good reason to.*

"All right, then," I said. "I'll put in a good word for you."

The server arrived and we ordered. Over dinner, my father filled me in on his last twenty years. After running out with Mom's money, he'd decided it would be better for everyone if he left town and got a fresh start somewhere else. He'd eventually worked his way down to Florida, with stints of a year or two doing odd jobs in various towns and cities in South Carolina and Georgia. He'd never married and had no more children.

"The longer I was gone," he said, "the harder it was for me to come back. I figured y'all were better off without me."

Truthfully? He was right. We had been better off without him, in the long run. But even though he'd said it, it wouldn't be nice to agree with him. He'd already figured that out for himself. Besides, just because we'd been better off with Mr. Yancey as our father figure, it didn't mean we'd come out of things unscathed, that we couldn't have benefitted from some type of relationship, however limited, with our biological father.

"Where are you staying here in town?" I asked.

He named a rundown motel known for cheap rates, cheap hookers, and an occasional bedbug infestation. No wonder he'd been in no hurry to get out of jail. "I went by my mother's place," he said. "Another family lives there now. Apparently, she passed on a few years ago. Lung cancer."

That's irony for you. I offered to help pay for an extended-stay hotel, but he wouldn't have it.

"You've done enough already," he said.

We walked out to our motorcycles, and parted ways with my promise to arrange a face-to-face between him, Mom, and Brie. I wasn't quite ready to hug him just yet. Still, when I climbed back onto my police bike, I felt strangely taller and lighter, unburdened and free. Trixie had been right, as usual. I sent her a text to let her know her guidance had been spot-on. *Had dinner with my father. Filled the fuck-it bucket.* I followed the message with a kissy-face emoji.

Chapter Eleven

The Buck Stops Here, Too

At half past midnight, a light drizzle began to fall. I rode my police bike back to the station and exchanged it for a cruiser. Riding a motorcycle was dicey enough under the best of conditions, but factor in rain-slick roads and poor visibility and riding the bike would be nothing short of perilous. I might be brave, but I wasn't crazy.

I'd just started the engine when my cell phone buzzed with an incoming text. I pulled it from the cup holder and checked the screen. The message was from Amberlyn. *Had a great time tonight! He's got a friend for you.*

After spending the day with Deputy Archer, I'd all but forgotten Amberlyn's promise to have her new romantic interest rustle up someone for me if her date went well. I supposed I should be excited about the prospect of meeting someone new, but I was more excited about my plans to perform further surveillance with Deputy Archer tomorrow. Maybe we could take our professional relationship to another level, add a personal element. He seemed interested, possibly. Still, I gave Amberlyn a thumbs-up in response. Better hedge my bets, right?

#

Luckily, the rain had moved on by the time I woke late Sunday morning. After showering and pulling my hair back in a pony tail, I slid my wallet and phone into the pouch on my belt, kissed Oscar on the cheek, and set out on my Harley. While small, shallow puddles remained along the sides of the road, the sun was out in full force this morning and had dried last night's rain off the roadways.

My GPS app led me to a one-story gray brick ranch home off Highway 920 about halfway between the towns of Pittsboro and Bear Creek. While the home was at least five decades old, it appeared to be well-maintained. It had black shutters and white trim, with two black rocking chairs on the front porch. It sat about fifty yards back from the road at the end of a driveway paved with asphalt, and was surrounded by a four-foot chain link fence. Zane's Sheriff's Department SUV sat under a metal carport that had been erected off to the side, outside the fence perimeter. A dark blue king-cab Ford pickup sat beside it. The bed contained a bright red two-person kayak. Yellow nylon rope secured the plastic vessel to metal cleats along the top of the truck bed.

I brought my motorcycle to a stop beside the car port, cut the engine, and removed my helmet. As I climbed off my bike, a big black dog rose from the porch and wagged his tail as he barked a friendly greeting. *Rrruff! Ruff-ruff!* The dog appeared to be mostly lab but with something shaggy mixed in. Having heard his dog announce my arrival, Zane opened the door and stepped outside. He wore a pair of cargo shorts and tennis shoes along with an untucked black T-shirt that accentuated the long, lean lines of his body.

As I walked through the gate, the dog came down the two steps from the porch and trotted over to greet me. Zane followed. I reached down and scratched the dog behind his ears, but apparently that wasn't good enough. He flopped over onto his back exposing a circle of white fur on his chest. He kicked his legs in the air and woofed, begging to have his belly scratched. I bent down and obliged the big beast, digging in with all ten fingers to make a good impression on him.

"That's Eight-ball." Zane gestured to the white spot on the black dog's chest. "I suppose it's obvious how he got his name."

"Because he's magic?" I teased, playing dumb.

"Well, he can make hot dogs disappear right before your very eyes."

The dog wriggled gleefully on his back as I scratched him. "Who's a good boy?" I asked. He responded by wagging his tail harder. *Me! I'm a good boy!*

I looked up at Zane. "Any word from Mrs. Tucker's son?"

"Yeah. He couldn't remember the tenant's full legal name, only that he goes by J.J. The guy pays his rent every month by money order. Brings it by and drops it off in person."

In other words, the tenant paid via a means that would be much harder to trace than a personal check or online transaction. Money orders were purchased with cash, and in most cases no identification was required to buy them. They weren't printed with the payer's information, either.

Zane added, "Tucker's son won't be able to tell us the guy's full name until he gets back from his trip and can access the lease. He said the guy was clean shaven when he first rented the place, but that he's since grown a beard."

So he could be the guy I'd seen in the security video from the medical center. Still, it would be easier if we knew for certain who lived at the property. We could check for a criminal record, or determine if he was some type of mechanic or involved with cars in some way. Without that information, we could be spitting in the wind here. All we really had to go on was that the guy had rented a property with an aluminum outbuilding big enough to house a car. That was pretty flimsy evidence, at best.

"Monday's recycle day," Zane said. "If the tenant puts a bin out, I'll take a look in it, see if there's any junk mail with his name on it."

"Good idea."

I stood and the dog flipped expertly over onto all fours and levered himself to a stand.

Zane reached down and ruffled his ears. "You've got to stay

here boy. Officer Sharpe is taking your place in the boat today."

He issued a soft whine as we closed the gate on him, but quieted when Zane pulled a large dog biscuit from his pocket and tossed it his way. Zane and I climbed into the truck.

I fastened my seatbelt and sniffed the air. "Is that gasoline I smell?"

He tilted his head to indicate the gas-powered leaf blower lying across the floorboard of the backseat. "I promised my mother I'd come by sometime this week to clear the leaves from her flowerbeds and garden. The smell reminds me I need to get over there."

"Can't you just put a reminder in your phone?"

"I can ignore a phone. I can't ignore that odor."

I waved a hand in front of my face. "Tell me about it."

Zane started his truck. "Let's grab a quick bite at the diner before we head out. I can't function without biscuits and gravy."

He'd get no argument from me. Once again, all I'd had before setting out this morning was a cup of coffee.

I kept an eye on our surroundings as we drove to the diner, making use of the drive to scout for the Barracuda. The roads were fairly busy with church traffic, as those who'd attended the early services were now leaving Sunday school and those who'd slept in were arriving for the late services. Zane raised his fingers from the wheel to wave to one of his fellow deputies who was standing in the roadway, directing traffic at the exit from a church parking lot.

"Poor guy," I said. "He must've drawn the short stick." Directing traffic was the worst. It was extremely dangerous, especially these days when everyone was distracted. I'd been grazed by a bumper a couple of times, and had nearly had my toes run over a dozen more.

There was no sign of the Barracuda. All I saw were family cars filled with folks dressed in their Sunday best, a few pickup trucks, a John Deere tractor, and a snazzy silver Chevy Camaro circa 2015 parked at the pumps of a gas station a quarter mile from the diner. *Nice ride.*

A white cargo van with an aluminum extension ladder secured to the top turned out of the diner's parking lot as we turned in. Two burly, bearded men in coveralls sat in the front seats, probably on their way to jobsite. Unfortunately, whatever spot they'd vacated had already been filled by one of the cars circling the lot. We drove around twice before being forced to park on the grass along the edge of the asphalt.

I climbed out of the truck. "Looks like everyone in the county is here right now."

Zane closed his door, too. "Sunday morning's their busiest time. Lucky for us, my mother keeps a table just for family in the back of the kitchen."

We stepped through the diner's door to find a crowd of people waiting to be seated and to see Pauline at the telephone by the register, frantically jabbing buttons. She put the phone to her ear and, an instant later, Zane's phone began whistling in his pocket as it launched into the theme song from *The Andy Griffith Show.* An appropriate ringtone as the late actor had played a sheriff in the show, which was set in a fictionalized version of his North Carolina hometown.

Zane pulled the phone from his pocket and tapped the screen to accept the call. "Hey, Mom." He paused a moment and raised a hand in the air. "Look up."

Pauline looked up, spotted Zane waving, and hung up the phone. She rushed over, squeezed through the crowd, and grabbed our shoulders, pulling us in close. "I think the man you've been looking for was just here!" She told us that the cashier had rung up the man's bill and noticed his beard was sparkling. "He'd called in a takeout order. He picked it up a few minutes ago and left."

My nerves began to sizzle like the hash browns on the grill. *We just might get the guy!*

Zane asked, "Did she see what kind of car he was driving? Maybe get a license plate?"

Pauline shook her head. "No. She said she tried, but he walked past the windows and then she couldn't see him anymore. His car must have been parked on the side or behind the building. She ran straight back to the kitchen to tell me. By the time I got through the crowd and out to the parking lot, he was nowhere in sight. I saw a couple of cars pull out of the lot, but they both headed west so all I could see was their back ends. I couldn't see who was in them. I asked the people waiting if they'd seen the man get into a car, but nobody had been looking out the windows. Nobody recognized him, either. They didn't seem to have paid him much mind."

They'd probably been too distracted by the display of pies in front of them. I know I would've been. Heck, I had a hard time not being distracted by them right now!

Zane glanced out the window behind us. "The cars that drove off. What types were they?"

"One was a green mini-van with a bunch of those family decals on the back window," Pauline said. "The other was a maroon, four-door Cadillac. The way it was poking along made me think one of our older customers must be driving it."

Neither vehicle sounded like one a classic car thief would be driving, assuming he had a choice in the matter.

Zane must have had the same thought. "We passed a work van with two men inside when we pulled into the diner. Wonder if he could've been one of them."

"Could be," I said. "They both had beards."

"Let's talk to the cashier right quick."

He strode up to the register and motioned the cashier aside. Pauline and I followed him.

The girl excused herself to the customer waiting at the counter and stepped over to speak privately with us. Zane said,

"Mom says you saw a man with a sparkly beard?"

"Mm-hm. They were black sparkles. Or maybe dark brown."

Uh-oh. "The same color as his beard, you mean?"

She nodded. "He was wearing a ball cap, and I didn't even notice until he lifted his chin and the light caught 'em."

My hopes faded a bit. Beards were big business, and stores sold all kinds of beard-care products. Beard oil. Beard conditioner. Beard balm. I'd even seen something called beard butter once. Any of those products might have added a shimmer to his natural color, and if he had some gray or silver hair in his beard, the effect might look like glitter or paint flecks. I asked about the hair on his head, whether it was salt and pepper, but she said his hat had covered it so she wasn't sure. She couldn't remember the color of his ball cap, and neither Zane nor I could remember whether either man in the cargo van had been wearing a cap. We'd only gotten a quick glimpse as we'd passed them.

Zane leaned toward her intently, as if by staring into her eyes he could visualize for himself the man that she had seen. "What else was he wearing besides the cap?"

"A black T-shirt with a pocket."

If he had been one of the men in the van, he could have donned the coveralls over his T-shirt after returning to the vehicle. But why not wait until they got to the jobsite? "Did he order enough for two people?" I asked.

"No," the cashier said. "Just a single two-egg omelet with a side of grits and a plain biscuit."

The fact that the man had ordered only enough for one person made it seem less likely that he'd been one of the guys in the van.

"How did he pay?" If the guy had used a credit or debit card, we could trace the number to his bank and get his name.

"Cash."

Damn. Zane and I exchanged a glance. His tight face told me he was as disappointed as I was. We couldn't be sure if the guy she'd rung up even had paint in his beard, and the fact that he'd ordered only one breakfast and wasn't wearing coveralls made it unlikely the man had been one of the two we'd seen in the van. Neither of us had seen which way they'd turned when they left the parking lot, either. *If only we'd gotten here a few minutes sooner . . .*

Zane thanked the cashier, and I did the same.

Pauline scoffed. "The guy didn't order gravy with his biscuits? What kind of self-respecting man doesn't want gravy with his biscuits?"

Zane raised his hands and pointed both thumbs back at himself. "Not this guy. Give me all the gravy you've got."

Pauline handed me a menu, but didn't bother to give one to her son. She angled her head to indicate the kitchen. "Head on back, you two. I'll be around in a minute."

Zane led me through the bustling kitchen to a small bistro set at the back, just inside the rear door. After deciding on biscuits and gravy with a side of fresh fruit, I watched the kitchen staff go about their duties. Though they worked at warp speed, they functioned like a well-oiled machine. As much grease as they used, it was no wonder they ran so smoothly. I'd never seen so much vegetable oil and shortening be put to use.

Pauline circled by to take our order, and filled it in under a minute, fixing our plates herself. "Enjoy, you two."

"Thanks!" As she hustled off, I turned back to Zane. "Wow. I've never gotten an order so fast."

Zane raised his fork in tribute. "It pays to have friends in high places."

Eager to get to to work, we made quick work of the delicious food, slid out the back door, and aimed for the county park. On the drive there, we passed Mrs. Tucker's property. Again, we saw little other than the glint off the aluminum roof of the outbuilding.

A quarter mile farther, we approached a double-wide mobile home set close to the road. Zane's gaze ventured off the road in front of us and past me, to the right, as we passed it. He pulled into the next driveway, came to a stop, and backed up to go back the way we'd come.

"See something?" I asked.

He pointed as we pulled up to the dirt drive of the mobile home. I followed his finger to see a rectangular device strapped to a tree. It had a round glass lens on the front.

"Is that some type of home security camera?" I asked.

"No. It's a trail cam. People put them out to capture photos of wildlife. Hunters use them to figure out where the game trails are."

No wonder I wasn't familiar with them. You couldn't shoot game within the Durham City limits, and neither my stepdad nor anyone else I knew was into hunting.

Zane pulled up the dirt drive and parked in front of the mobile home. A tire swing hung from a tree and a square sandbox sat in the yard, with colorful plastic buckets and shovels strewn about the sand. A playhouse made to look like a log cabin stood under a tall pine amidst a scattering of dried needles the tree had shed. Parked on the other side of the drive were a white Subaru hatchback and a blue Dodge sedan. Two children's booster seats were strapped in the backseat of the Subaru. The back bumpers of both vehicles were decorated with bumper stickers. *Coexist. Don't Hate, Meditate. Be the Change You Want to See in the World. Bernie 2016. Bernie 2020.*

I followed Zane up onto the porch. He rapped on the door. A moment later, a woman's voice called out inside. "It's the sheriff!"

A thirtyish woman yanked the door open. She sported a worried expression, along with red hair and an explosion of freckles across her face and arms. The twin boys hanging onto her legs sported the same hair, like duplicate, miniature Ed Sheerans. *What a couple of cuties.* They looked to be around four years old, their toddler chubbiness gone but all their baby teeth still in place.

A man with shaggy blond hair stepped up behind the woman and addressed us over her shoulder. "Is something wrong, Deputy?"

Zane raised his palms in a no-need-to-worry gesture. "It's all good." He introduced both himself and me. "We're working an investigation in the area and happened to notice you've got a trail camera on your tree out front."

The woman put her hands atop her boys' heads and ruffled their hair. "These two love to watch the wildlife. We put up the camera so the boys can see what comes through the yard at night or when we're not looking."

One of the boys chimed in, his eyes wide with excitement. "We saw a bear!"

"A bear!" Zane repeated, matching the boy's enthusiasm. "That's so cool!"

The father filled us in on the camera's workings. "We paid a little extra to get the wireless model. It records up to sixty seconds of video at a time. We go through the videos every week or so and only keep the good stuff."

I glanced back at the device. "Does it pick up activity on the road?"

"Only cars heading south," the man said. "The range doesn't extend to the far lane."

Luckily for me and Zane, the Tucker place sat south of this property. If the Barracuda had been driven past this family's home on its way to the Tucker's, it should show up on the recordings. Assuming, of course, that the camera had been running at the time. "Is the camera on all day?" I asked.

The man nodded. "Twenty-four seven."

Zane pointed a finger into their home. "Any chance we can come in and take a look at the feed?"

"No problem." The man waved us inside and led us over to a desktop computer. He took a seat in the desk chair and gave us a quick lesson in how to operate the feed.

One of the boys tugged on his father's T-shirt. "Show them the bear, Daddy!"

"Yeah!" the other said. "Show them the bear!"

The man cut a look to Zane and me. We didn't have a lot of time to spare, but how could we disappoint the excited little boys?

"I'd love to see the bear," I said.

"Me, too," Zane agreed.

The man pulled up the video. The screen showed their yard dappled with early morning sunlight, slivers of sun just beginning to peek through the woods as it rose over a far-off horizon. The time stamp in the lower corner indicated the video clip was recorded a week prior at 6:48 AM. As we watched, a medium-sized black bear ambled out of the woods and looked around the driveway.

"That bear's up early," I said. "He must've been looking for breakfast."

Zane looked down at the boys. "Think he likes pancakes or waffles better?"

"Pancakes!" hollered one.

"Waffles!" shouted the other.

Their mother cringed. "Inside voices, boys!"

The bear wandered about, occasionally raising his tan-colored snout like a dog to sniff the air. When he neither found nor scented anything he might eat for breakfast, he returned to the edge of the woods. There, he raised his short tail, popped a slight squat, and released a barrage of bear droppings onto the ground.

Zane's head bobbed as he watched. "This video answers the proverbial question. We now know for certain where bears defecate and it is, indeed, in the woods." He looked down at the boys. "That was cool. Thanks for having your dad show it to us."

Our review of the bear video complete, the man stood and offered Zane the chair, then went to the kitchen and rounded up a seat for me. Zane played with the feed to show what it had recorded on late Monday morning. Sure enough, right around the time I'd been swerving to avoid the buck, a lime-green car crossed the frame. Given that the driveway was narrow and flanked by trees, the car was on the screen for a mere instant before it disappeared again.

Zane dragged the circle at the bottom to take the feed back a few seconds, and froze it when the car appeared. Between the velocity of the vehicle and the limited resolution of the video, we couldn't say with absolute certainty that the bright blur was the Barracuda, but the odds of another car the same color as the 'Cuda passing this way at that time seemed small.

"Looks like we're on the right track," I said.

Zane squinted at the screen as if that would somehow make the blurry image more clear. "Seems that way. But just because the car drove past here doesn't mean it's still in the area."

Party pooper. I scowled at him. "I know that. But if it's not, that means the Chatham County Sheriff's Department let a car thief slip through its fingers."

"Back to the blame game, are we?"

Ignoring his jibe, I pulled my phone from my pocket. I'd snapped photos of the police reports on each of the thefts. The most recent theft before the Barracuda was the Bel Air. According to the report, the car was stolen on a Wednesday, five days prior to the theft of the Barracuda. I mentally computed how long it might take for a car thief to drive from the Wellborn home to our current location, assuming he was driving within the speed limits. *Twenty, maybe twenty-five minutes?* I gestured to the screen. "See if they've still got footage from April ninth starting at 2:20 AM." I held my breath, hoping the couple hadn't erased it yet.

Zane rolled the mouse and tapped the keyboard until he accessed the feed. "Looks like there's something here."

He played the footage. On screen, the porch light illuminated a small area of the driveway and the woods behind it. Movement in the woods caused the camera to activate. As I watched, a deer with short, velvety antlers stepped out of the trees and into the open. His ears pricked up and rotated as if seeking the source of a faint sound. He turned to stare at the camera.

"Oh, my gosh!" I said. "It's him again!"

Zane looked at the screen before cocking his head. "Who?"

"That's the same buck that ran me off the road." I pointed. "See? His antlers look like someone giving the finger."

Zane squinted again at the screen. "You're right."

As we watched, the buck walked right up to the camera and looked into it, as if issuing another challenge. After staring us down for a few seconds, he turned his head and walked away, flicking his tail dismissively. At the edge of the driveway, lights flashed as a car went by.

I hit the button to pause the feed. Again, the image was blurry from the movement. Add in the dark of the night, and the image was even less clear. Even so, the signature bubble shape of the car's roof and the wide stripes of the whitewall tires were discernable. "It's the Bel Air. It has to be."

We looked to see if footage had been retained from the dates of the earlier thefts, but there was none on the computer. When we were done with our review, we asked the man to forward copies of the relevant video clips to our e-mail addresses. We stood by to watch while he sent the videos, and checked the e-mail attachments on our phones to make sure we could view the footage.

"Got it," I said.

Zane concurred. We made note of the man's contact information in case we needed to get in touch, thanked him for his cooperation, and off to the lake we went.

Chapter Twelve

Row, Row, Row Your Boat

Buoyed by the corroborating evidence that the stolen cars had traveled the road on which the Tucker property sat, we pulled into the recreation area. There, we slipped out of the truck and into bright orange life vests. Thanks to my oversized bust, I had to extend the straps as far as they would go to be able to close the snaps. A smile played about Zane's mouth when he noticed, but he was smart enough not to comment. Despite the fact that I avoided tight, low-cut shirts, I'd heard more than enough comments about my big breasts from boys and men over the years. *Jerks.* It sucked to be reduced to one body part. I was so much more than that. My smile was nice, too. But, of course, in my opinion, my perky personality was my best selling point.

Zane pulled a small tube of sunscreen from the pocket of his shorts. "Heads up." He tossed the tube to me.

I squirted a generous dollop into my hand before tossing it back to him. "You better slather up those white legs of yours. They look like they've never seen the sun."

He wagged his brows. "Noticed my legs, did you?" He struck a pose, one hand on his hip, the other in his hair, and tossed his head back, lips parted, as if he were on a photo shoot for a Victoria's Secret catalog. "What else have you noticed?'

"That you have absolutely no shame."

Properly outfitted and protected from UV exposure, we grabbed the handles at either end of the kayak and carried it down a leaf-strewn embankment where we could launch the boat from shore.

He handed me one of the long paddles. "Sit in the front. I'll push it off."

I took a seat in the front of the kayak and slid my legs into the empty space in the hull. I held the paddle up as Zane pushed the boat forward. The bottom scraped on twigs and rocks until it was far enough into the water that it began to float. Zane slipped into the seat behind me in one smooth, easy motion, as if he'd done this a thousand times before. As he did, a tennis ball rolled back from inside the hull and bumped softly against the seat. I picked it up. "Looks like Eight-ball forgot his toy."

Zane reached over my shoulder and took it from me. "I can throw it out in the water for you to fetch if you'd like."

Looking back over my shoulder at him, I brandished my paddle. "Don't make me come back there."

My gaze roamed the shore, seeking something to give me some bearings. While I'd been out on Jordan Lake several times throughout my life, it had been a couple of years since the last time, and I didn't know the water well. The shoreline all looked the same to me. Trees, trees, and more trees. "Where to?"

"I looked over satellite maps online last night." Zane raised his arm and pointed to a spot at approximately the 2:00 position. "See where that water tower is? That's where we're headed."

"All right," I said. "Full speed ahead."

We turned slightly and paddled along, inadvertently knocking our oars a few times before we fell into rhythm together. The water gave off a soft *shush-shush-shush* as we paddled our way across the lake, an occasional wave sending up a light spray of water onto my face and arms. The sky was sunny and cloudless, and the cool droplets provided a welcome, if brief, respite from the day's heat before they dried.

As we moved along, Zane launched into a sea shanty, singing with a deep timbre. "Come all ya young fellers that follow the sea—"

I'd learned the song in music class as a child and joined in with him on the chorus. "Way, hey, blow the man down."

Zane sang alone again, "Now just pay attention and listen to me."

Together we bellowed, "Give me some time to blow the man down."
"Aboard the Black Baller I first served my time."
He let me sing the chorus alone this time. "With a way, hey, blow the man down,
"But on the Black Baller I wasted my prime."
"Give me some time to blow the man down."
After ten minutes of paddling, we drew close to the shore.

"Land ho!" Zane called. "Raise your oar."

I lifted my oar out of the water and he expertly banked the craft. I climbed out onto the marshy land and grabbed the handle, pulling the kayak farther up until he could disembark without having to step into the water. We set the oars down next to the boat, and took off our life jackets. It would be difficult to perform clandestine surveillance in a day-glow orange vest.

"Are we allowed to be here?" I asked. If we were on the Tucker's property, we'd need a search warrant. Even though Elsie Tucker owned the place, she didn't have the authority to grant us access given that the place was subject to a binding lease. Only the current tenant could legally allow us onto the property without a search warrant. We had to be careful. The last thing we wanted was any evidence we collected being thrown out on the grounds of illegal search and seizure.

"We're okay," Zane assured me. "I checked things out. The Army Corps of Engineers owns this stretch of land adjacent to the lake. The Tucker place is fenced, so we'll know when we get there."

In other words, we'd have a visible boundary. *Good.*

Zane led the way into the woods, occasionally stopping and putting his field glasses to his eyes to try to better get his bearings. Eventually, we came to the fence at the back of Mrs. Tucker's property. The fence was a rail and wire style, formed by thick chicken wire supported by vertical and horizontal wood rails. NO TRESPASSING signs had been erected every thirty feet or so along the top rail. From the relatively new look of the signs, they'd been put up recently.

Zane pointed off to our right, where we could see the house and storage building through the trees. As we made our way along the fence, we hunkered down to be less visible in case the tenant was home and happened to look out a back window. The metal building we'd spotted earlier sat close to the back of the acreage, and we could get a good look at it from here. Unfortunately, the doors on it were closed and padlocked.

I raised my binoculars to my eyes and scanned the property. Parked in front of the house was a silver Chevy Camaro, facing us. *Could it be the same Camaro I saw at the gas station near Pauline's Diner earlier?* I couldn't be certain. North Carolina law required official license plates only on the rear of vehicles, and many people opted to put novelty plates on the front. The owner of this car had done just that. The plate featured two black and white checkered flags on crossed poles, the flags extended to either side as if waving. They were the type of flags used at raceways, such as the Charlotte Motor Speedway. Could this mean something? Or was it coincidence? "Check out the license plate on the car," I told Zane.

He raised his field glasses to his eyes. "He's a racing fan."

A sound drew our attention to the back door of the house. As the door banged open, I dove to the ground behind a tree. Zane did the same, landing on top of me. *Oof!*

Though his full weight was pressed against my back and legs, Zane couldn't move or he'd risk the guy spotting us. Zane put his mouth to my ear and whispered "sorry," his breath warm on my neck. Given that he had me pinned to the moist dirt of the forest floor, I really shouldn't have found the situation so enjoyable.

Had the man seen us back here? We waited a few beats to see if he would shout or come to the fence. When neither happened, Zane eased off my back to kneel and peer surreptitiously around the tree trunk. I levered myself to a crouch next to him and spied from the other side of the trunk. The man walked to the barn and fingered through a set of keys before inserting one into the padlock. One twist and the lock came open, the chain falling free.

Zane and I exchanged eager glances as the man went to open the door to the outbuilding. Would we see the Barracuda inside? Maybe the Bel Air or Aston Martin? I held my breath and crossed my fingers, sending up a silent prayer to the heavens to help me find Jerry Beaumont's prized vehicle and put a smile back on the sick old man's face.

To my dismay, when the man opened the metal barn, all he revealed was several large cardboard boxes, assorted lawn equipment, and camping gear, including a red kerosene lantern, a gas cook stove, and a bundle of collapsed tan canvas that appeared to be a tent. No Aston Martin. No Bel Air. No Barracuda. There were no tell-tale splotches of dripped paint on the concrete floor, no spray residue on the inside walls, just a rake leaning innocently against the wall. The guy walked to a wooden workbench, grabbed a reusable water bottle he'd apparently forgotten there, and came back out, locking the doors behind him. Rather than return to the house, he circled around it, climbed into his car, and started the engine. He whipped around in a quick circle and disappeared down the driveway, the house blocking our view of him now.

"Did you get his license plate number?" Zane asked.

I'd managed only a split-second glimpse of the back of his car before he'd headed off. "Did it start with a D?"

"I thought it was an O."

The two letters could look alike from a distance. "Darn."

Zane shrugged. "I suppose it doesn't much matter. It didn't look like he's using the barn for painting or hiding cars. I think we can cross him off our list of suspects."

I exhaled sharply. "But he was the *only* person on our list of suspects."

"Then I guess we can throw the list away."

"Ugh. We've been barking up the wrong tree." I banged my forehead lightly against the tree I'd been hiding behind. As I did, my eyes spotted several stacks of firewood and mountainous piles of dried leaves past the boathouse, at the edge of the woods. With so many trees around the property, it was certain several would fall or lose limbs each year, providing a ready source of firewood. The dense trees provided no shortage of dead leaves in the winter, too. Some people raked them up for composting, but many more, especially those in rural areas like this, simply let the leaves lie where they fell. Gathering them up was time-consuming, backbreaking work. *Why would the tenant bother?*

The stacks of chopped wood surrounded the leaf piles on three sides. Orange plastic netting had been stretched across the fourth side where it would help keep the leaves corralled but could easily be rolled back so that additional leaves could be added to the piles. Most of the leaf piles were long and tall, standing three or four feet high at their pinnacle, but one was even slightly taller, around five feet by my best estimate.

I returned my binoculars to my eyes. The tallest leaf pile, which stood at the back of the makeshift pen, looked different somehow. The texture wasn't quite the same as the rest of the pile, nor were the colors. They were both slightly off, weren't they? What's more, there were still plenty of dead leaves lying about the yard area. It didn't appear to have been fully raked. Had the tenant tired and given up on the job halfway through, or had he stopped collecting the leaves because he'd accomplished what he'd set out to do—hiding a stolen car in a place he thought nobody would think to check?

Think again, buddy.

I jerked my head to indicate the pile. "Check out those leaves. Something look strange to you?"

Zane peered through his glasses for a long moment. "No.

What caught your eye?"

"The tallest pile at the back. It's a slightly different color and the pattern of the leaves is different somehow."

He squinted. "I suppose you're right. But maybe it's an older pile, at a different phase of decomposition."

I took another look. "That pile is about the size of a car. Just sayin'."

"Who would hide a car under leaves?" he said, both his voice and face strained with skepticism. "One good wind and they'd blow away."

"One good wind," I repeated, "and we could see if there's anything underneath them."

Zane gazed up at the motionless trees. "Too bad it's a still day."

"Hmm." I crossed my arms over my chest and thoughtfully tapped my chin with my index finger. "If only we had access to some sort of device that blows air."

"I could take off my shirt and wave it," Zane suggested.

I had to admit, I wouldn't mind seeing the guy without a shirt on. "That's not exactly what I had in mind."

"Did you mean a hair dryer?" Zane said, scratching his head. "Or a box fan? We'd have to drag a generator out here. An extension cord, too."

"I really hope you're just playing dumb."

He chuckled and motioned for me to follow him. "Back to the kayak."

We returned the boat and paddled fast and hard back to his truck. He snatched the leaf blower from the cab and came back to the boat. "Spread your legs."

I eyed him from under accusing brows. "Excuse me?"

"My legs take up too much space. It'll fit better up here with you."

"All right." I spread my legs, resting my knees against the inside of the hold. He slid the leaf blower between my knees, resting the handle on the end of my seat directly between my thighs. The leaf blower extended out in front of me like some type of oversized mechanical phallus.

In seconds, we were off again, paddling fast and furious across the lake.

My back, upper arms, and wrists ached from the repetitive rowing motion, but I was determined to give it my all. I worried that the stream of air from the leaf blower might not be forceful enough to move the leaves, but we had no other option. We couldn't very well ask a judge to issue a search warrant based on such flimsy evidence as a large pile of leaves.

We went ashore in the same spot as before, but this time we walked farther down the fence to get as close to the leaf piles as we could while remaining on public land. We checked to make sure the Camaro was still gone, and crossed our fingers that nobody else was in the house who might overhear us out here.

Zane pulled the string on the leaf blower and it revved up with a roar, sending up a spray of dead leaves, pine needles, and dirt. While I covered my ears, he turned and aimed the nozzle at the closest leaf pile, which stood a dozen feet from the fence and blocked the bigger leaf pile at the back. The forced air went through the safety netting and a couple of downed acorns rolled away, but nothing much else happened. *Damn!* Unfortunately, the canopy of trees overhead let little direct sunlight shine down on the area. The leaves remained damp from last night's rain, weighted down with moisture.

"Wave it back and forth!" I hollered to Zane. "Maybe it will dry them out."

He tried my suggestion. Slowly, bit by bit, the pile dried enough so that chunks of leaves broke free and blew off to the sides of the enclosure. Finally, the odd pile at the back was exposed. He aimed the nozzle at the top of it. Rather than blowing away, it seemed to merely ruffle in the wind. He turned to me, a puzzled look on his face, before turning back. I nudged him with my elbow and pointed at the bottom of the heap. He shrugged, but aimed the blast of air at the lower part of the stack, where leaves met earth. The pile lifted a few inches, hovering on the current. Only it wasn't a leaf pile. It was camouflage netting, like the kind the army used to obscure tanks and other equipment on military bases. Hunters sometimes used the netting, too, to hide themselves from their prey.

Something's under that net. Something the tenant doesn't want us to see.

Zane lowered the leaf blower until it was nearly on the ground and put it right up against the wire fencing for maximum impact. The netting blew up just far enough for us to get a peek at a black tire, an exhaust pipe, and a shiny chrome bumper.

I was right! There's a car under there! But was it one of the stolen cars?

Zane gestured to my fanny pack before raising his free hand to his face and miming a picture-taking motion. He was right. We'd need a photo of the car, or as much of it as we could manage to reveal, in order to get a search warrant for the property. I pulled my phone from the pack and bent down to best be able to capture a pic.

He waved the blower back and forth and the netting lifted again. This time, it revealed not only the tire, bumper, and exhaust pipe, but part of the license plate. UDA. I captured the image with my camera before the net settled back into place. The plate on Jerry Beaumont's car was DV CUDA. *It has to be his car, doesn't it?*

Zane jerked the blower in an upward motion this time, and the netting blew up to reveal not only enough of the license plate for us to see it read CUDA, but also a couple inches of lime-green paint. I snapped another quick picture and stood. Zane and I exchanged a high five and I threw victorious fists in the air.

Busted!

Chapter Thirteen

Wild Ride

Zane turned off the leaf blower. "Let's hustle. We've got to move before the guy gets home and notices that someone's messed with his leaf piles. I'll round up a search warrant while you run home and change into your uniform."

What a nice change of pace. Most guys tried to get me out of my clothes, not into them.

Zane and I sprinted through the forest on our way back to the kayak. We paddled furiously once more, loaded the kayak in the bed of his pickup, and raced out of the park.

Back at Zane's place, I hopped out of the truck and ran for my motorcycle while he ran for his porch.

"Meet me back at the Tucker's property!" he called.

I slid my helmet on and cranked my engine, zipping down Zane's driveway and back onto the main road. I rode as fast as I dared back to my apartment, where I exchanged my civilian clothes for my uniform and my Harley for my BMW police bike. I phoned Detective Mulaney and quickly told him about the recent developments. "Okay if I help the Chatham County Sheriff's Department nab the guy?"

"Hell, yeah, if they'll have you. You've earned this bust."

"Thanks, Mule."

In less than an hour, I was back at the Tucker place, motoring down the long drive. I pulled up to find Zane's SUV parked in front of the house. *Has he already arrested the car thief?* I hoped I hadn't missed all the fun.

A glance around told me the Camaro wasn't on site. The tenant had yet to return. Heaven help us if he'd noticed us spying from the woods behind his house or otherwise gotten wind of our investigation and taken off. We might never find him.

I parked my motorcycle next to the SUV and looked to the left to see that Zane had pulled the camouflage netting all the way back, revealing Jerry Beaumont's Barracuda. I walked over to take a closer look.

Zane ran a hand over the hood. "This is one cherry car."

"When we tell Mr. Beaumont we found it for him, I'm sure he'll offer to take us for a ride."

"Think he'll let me drive it?"

"Not on your life. He only lets his wife drive it."

"Can't blame him."

Zane held up a pair of bolt cutters. "Let's take a closer look at the barn."

We circled around to the back of the house and stepped up to the door of the metal building. Zane spread the handles and positioned the blades around the heavy-duty chain to cut it. With a *clunk* and *jangle*, the chain broke and fell to the ground, pooling on the dirt. Zane leaned the bolt cutters against the outside of the building and pulled the door open.

We walked inside, both of us donning latex gloves so as not to leave our fingerprints about the place. He stopped in front of one of the trunks and opened the lid. Inside was a full-face ventilated mask, the type used for large painting jobs or handling hazardous chemicals. A few small dots of metallic blue paint were visible along the rubber trim.

I ventured over to the canvas tent and lifted up on the roof bracket. It took enough shape for me to realize it was a pop-up work tent. While the outside was relatively spotless, the inside bore tell-tale signs of not only the blue metallic paint, but also red and black paint as well. The car thief had been smart to use the tent to prevent the evidence of his crimes from ending up on the walls and floor of the Tucker's boathouse. A pair of white hooded coveralls with small spots of paint spray splatter lay folded up inside the tent. Zane pointed to a container of auto paint in a burgundy color called Moulin Rouge. Looked like the thief had been just about to repaint the Barracuda. Good thing we'd found it before he'd finished the job.

Screeeee! The squeal of tires met our ears.

"He's back!" I yelled.

We ran out of the building to see the Camaro speeding off down the driveway, leaving behind a cloud of smoke. The acrid odor of burnt rubber involuntary crinkled our noses. *Damn!* We'd been stupid not to have one of us keep a lookout.

I could get my motorcycle moving much faster than Zane could get his SUV in motion. I ran to my bike. "Call backup!" I shouted to Zane as I leaped onto my ride. "I'll follow him!"

I slung a leg over the seat, started the engine, and was down the driveway in a flash. My head snapped to the left. *No Camaro.* I turned to look right. *There he is!*

I cranked back on the accelerator and rocketed out onto the roadway. I flipped on my lights and siren and leaned forward instinctively, as if to close the distance between me and the thief all the faster. He disappeared around a bend, but came into sight again once I'd rounded the curve myself.

In my mirror, I could see Zane behind me. He had less maneuverability on these winding roads in his SUV. Good thing I had my bike. Even a souped-up sports car like the thief's Camaro couldn't outrun me.

The thief hooked a sharp right turn onto another road, nearly spinning out before gaining purchase and zooming off. I braked and banked tight, my knee only inches off the pavement. Any lower and the asphalt would scrape the skin from my bones. My body moved at one with the bike, shifting into an upright position as we straightened out again.

The guy took another turn, this time to the left. When we were back on a straightaway, Zane leveled off his speed, maintaining a constant distance behind me for safety. But as the road tapered the Camaro executed another turn, this one onto the narrow shoulder. Red brake lights flashed as he slowed and hooked a turn directly in front of me to go back in the direction we'd come. I executed the about-face easily, but in his oversized SUV, Zane had to make a three-point turn and lost momentum again, lagging way behind now. *It's up to me to catch this classic-car-stealing bastard.*

As I edged closer, the driver's side window came down on the Camaro and a closed hand came out. It opened with a flourish, as if the driver were performing a jazz dance a la Caberet, and tossed a handful of loose change into the air. *PING! PING! PING!* A bombardment of coins rained down on me, pinging off my helmet and cracking both my windshield and the left side of my goggles. The bastard threw out another handful of loose change. The coins hit me like shrapnel from a bomb, my right arm, left boob, and left leg taking direct hits. *Damn, that hurts! This guy could kill me!*

Lest he have more change in his car, I backed off a bit. He turned again down a side road, and I made the turn a few seconds after him. In my mirrors, I saw Zane's SUV drive past the turn, then back up. But he was way behind now.

The driver turned again, then again, and now Zane was nowhere to be seen.

"Where are you?" he hollered over the radio, which I'd turned to the Chatham County Sheriff's Department frequency.

"I don't know!" I shouted back. It's not like I had time to

stop and read the road signs.

The guy's hand came out the window again, this time clutching the blue and white jacket he'd been wearing in the video when he'd stolen the Barracuda. He tossed the jacket into the air and it unfurled, large and light, floating in the air as if waiting for me. *Shit!* I slowed and swerved, but the damn thing seemed to follow me. The jacket came down right across my face, the sleeves wrapping around behind my helmet like a blindfold, flapping in the wind. *Flap-flap-flap!*

I reached up my left hand and fought with the fabric, eventually pulling the jacket free from the forces holding it in place. I hurled it aside and looked down the road. The Camaro was nowhere to be seen. The road curved ahead after another intersection. Had he continued straight? Turned left? Turned right? *ARGHHHH!*

I slowed as I approached the intersection and looked both ways, my vision impeded by my cracked goggle lens. I closed my left eye and looked only through my right. The road curved in both directions, disappearing behind the trees. Where had he gone?

After radioing my position to Zane and our backup, I scanned for clues. A swirl of dust and leaves settling on the pavement told me he'd turned to the right. I did the same. When I came around the curve, I saw the tail end of the Camaro go around yet another bend. *Damn these curvy roads and damn these woods!* While I loved them when out for a pleasure ride, they were doing nothing for me today other than impeding my arrest. I needed some help out here or this guy would get away!

I banked around the bend and *Hallelujah*, there was the help I needed. The buck with the finger-flipping antlers blocked the road ahead of the Camaro. While the driver might not care if he killed the deer, he was risking his own life if he didn't avoid a collision. He knew it, too. He swerved onto the shoulder, hit loose leaves and pine needles, and lost control. The car slid straight into the trunk of a solid old oak. *BAM!*

The airbag deployed, a white puff visible through the driver's open window. I slowed and pulled in behind the car. The buck ambled safely to the other side of the road, but stopped at the edge of the woods to watch.

I slid off my bike and ran to the window, readying my gun as I went. I reached the window just as the guy managed to fight his airbag back. He looked up to see me smiling down at him, my gun pointed at his chest.

"Hello, there," I said. "Thanks for the loose change. Most people don't think to tip their public servants."

He groaned and muttered a series of choice expletives.

I gestured with my gun. "Hands up. You're going to get out and kneel on the ground, or you're getting a bullet in your nards. Got me?"

He snorted derisively. "Loud and clear."

I opened his door and backed away as he stepped outside. He eyed me before looking about, as if evaluating his chances of escaping through the woods.

"Don't even think about it," I spat.

He looked around again, clearly still thinking about it despite my order not to.

"Down on your knees!" I commanded. "Now!"

But rather than get to his knees, he took off running toward the woods. I ran after him and leaped up onto his back to take him down. Only he didn't go down. He ended up taking me for a piggyback ride. I clung to him, one arm wrapped around his neck, the other keeping my gun held up to avoid accidentally shooting one of us.

He attempted to buck me off him by throwing his hips backward, but I held on tighter, my elbow crooked in a chokehold around his neck. Not easy with my large breasts wedged against his back, forming an obstacle between us. But I pulled tighter, grimacing against the pain in my injured boob. While the thief had refused to drop to his knees earlier, he did so involuntarily now due to a lack of oxygen. I was riding him to the ground when Zane's SUV pulled to a stop behind my bike.

As the man lay facedown on the dirt, gasping for air, I shoved my gun back into my holster, pulled his hands back, and cuffed him. *Click-click.*

Busted.

Chapter Fourteen

On the Road Again

The thief successfully detained, I turned to look at the buck. I bowed my head, silently thanking him for his assistance in the takedown. The buck blinked and bowed his head in return before slowly turning away and disappearing into the woods.

Zane hopped out of his vehicle, his brows raised, impressed. "Damn, woman. You don't mess around."

He grabbed the car thief by the arm to help him up. The guy refused to stand, hanging limply, making himself dead weight.

"Have it your way," Zane said. He grabbed the waistband of the guy's jeans with his free hand and dragged him over dirt, leaves, and pinecones until they reached the SUV. By then, the guy's eyes and nose were full of natural debris and he was feeling a little more cooperative. He stood and allowed himself to be buckled into the backseat of the SUV.

Zane slammed the door on the guy before turning to me. "You and I make a darn good team."

"Does that mean you'll give me some credit for the arrest? Even though I'm working under your authority?"

"After all you've done, I'd be one hell of a jackass to rob you of your glory."

"You're one hell of a jackass, regardless."

"Yeah, but you've enjoyed working with me." He narrowed his eyes at me. "Admit it."

I shrugged. "I guess it wasn't that bad."

He gave me a grin and a nod. "All right then. I'll report this like it was, a joint effort between Durham PD and the Chatham County Sheriff's Department."

#

The car thief wouldn't talk, but after booking him into the Chatham County lockup, Zane and I huddled in his SUV in the jail's parking lot and took a look at the guy's phone. We would have never got a password out of the guy but, luckily for us, he'd activated fingerprint access and we'd been able to open it with a touch of his thumb.

His apps, text messages, and e-mails helped us piece many of the clues together. He hadn't had an accomplice after all. He'd ordered magnetic GPS tracking devices online and surreptitiously placed them on the vehicles he'd been interested in so that he could monitor their locations. When a car was in an opportune place at an opportune time, he'd summoned an Uber and been dropped off a quarter mile or so from the target vehicle, within easy walking distance.

We returned to his rental house to gather evidence, including the pop-up painting tent, the painting mask, an airless paint sprayer, and the container of Moulin Rouge paint. Inside the house, we found a copy of a rental agreement for a storage unit down the road in Fayetteville. We called the city's police department, and they dispatched an officer who confirmed that the Bel Air was parked inside. It had been repainted, but was otherwise no worse for the wear. Presumably, the other vehicles had been sold or stored elsewhere, but the Mule would take the case from here. I had no doubt he'd get to the bottom of things. Further investigation was well above my pay grade, and would involve mostly paperwork and phone calls, tasks I'd be happy to leave to the detective.

Zane and I walked over to the Barracuda and stared at it for a long moment.

I sighed. "I suppose I should call the Beaumonts to come pick it up."

"I suppose you should." Zane's mouth spread in a mischievous grin. "But it would be a lot more fun to drive it."

I felt a grin on my lips, too. "And it would only be courteous to return the car to them at their home rather than forcing them to make the drive out here."

"Of course," he agreed. "It's the least we could do."

"We?"

"Joint operation," he reminded me. "We should each get a chance at the wheel."

"Can't argue with that logic."

"We should also go out to dinner afterwards to celebrate. Someplace fancy with cloth napkins and wines we can't pronounce. We earned it." He cocked his head and raised a brow in question.

"Can't argue with that logic, either."

The Barracuda hadn't been repaired since being hot-wired and, after watching a YouTube tutorial, we were able to start it without the key and without electrocuting ourselves. We left Zane's SUV and my police bike at the Tucker place. Zane drove the first leg back to Durham.

When we passed the sign marking the border between Chatham and Durham counties, I said, "You're in my jurisdiction now, buddy. Pull over."

We switched seats, and I drove the rest of the way to the Beaumonts' house.

Brody Riddle was out front playing basketball with friends

again as we pulled into the Beaumonts' driveway. He passed the ball to a friend and jogged over, a big smile on his face. "You found it!"

I pointed to the Beaumonts' front door. "You want to get Mr. Beaumont for me?"

"Yeah!" The kid ran to the door and banged on it.

A moment later, Gilda answered the door. She looked at Brody and he merely pointed to the driveway, where Deputy Archer and I stood next to the Barracuda, beaming with pride at our successful bust. Her hands went to her mouth in glee before she removed them and clapped them together. She turned and called back into the house. "Jerry! Come to the door! There's something you need to see!"

A few seconds later, Jerry ambled up on his walker. He hooted when he saw the car in the drive and danced a quick jig before he lost his balance and had to return his hands to the device. He came out the door and down the walk at surprising speed, a happy tear coursing down his cheek. "My baby! I never thought I'd see you again!" He ran a loving hand over the fender before kissing his hand and applying the kiss to the metal. He looked up at me and Zane. "I owe you two a kiss, too!"

"Thanks," Zane said on a chuckle, "but your gratitude is enough."

"I'll take one." I gave the man a hug and he kissed my cheek. "The ignition will have to be repaired," I told him. "It's still hot-wired."

"At least she's back where she belongs." He turned to Brody. "You know what, son? Life's too short not to share as much joy as possible. As soon as I get this car fixed, you and me are going for a ride. You're driving."

Brody's mouth gaped, his eyes bright with excitement. "Really?"

Jerry nodded. "Really."

#

Amberlyn was kind enough to give Zane and me a ride back to the Durham limits, where one of Zane's fellow deputies picked us up. As I slid out of the passenger seat of her patrol car, she reached out and grabbed my arm to stop me. She cast a glance back at Zane, who had just climbed out of the backseat behind her and closed the door. "I'm guessing you won't be needing me to set you up, after all?"

I surreptitiously shook my head and sent her a soft smile.

#

Two hours later, I was back at my apartment, my police bike in its usual spot on the runner next to my Harley. I'd cleaned myself up and slipped into a flirty blue dress and heels. I'd curled my hair and put on a full face of makeup. Zane had never seen this girly side of me. I was curious how he'd react.

When a knock sounded at my door, I opened it to find him wearing dress loafers, navy slacks, and a neatly pressed striped button-down. He held a bouquet of pink and white roses in his hands. His eyes flashed with appreciation and surprise before he leaned in to look past me. "I'm here for Shae. She around here somewhere?"

I twirled once and raised my palms. "You didn't think I'd clean up this good, did you?"

He handed me the flowers, a twinkle in his eye. "I'm not taking that bait. There's no response to that question that won't get me in trouble."

I carried the bouquet to the kitchen. Oscar jumped up onto the counter to inspect the blooms while I arranged the flowers in a glass vase with water.

Zane wagged a finger at the cat, who playfully swiped back at it. "Don't go knocking that vase off the counter."

We drove to my favorite Italian restaurant, where we enjoyed a three-course meal, topped off with a delicious tiramisu. We wrapped up the dinner with glasses of champagne.

Zane raised his glass flute in toast. "To the best law enforcement officers in the bi-county area."

I clinked my glass against his. "Hear, hear!"

Back at my apartment, Zane and I discovered that Oscar had torn several leaves off one of the roses before apparently being pricked by a thorn and deciding to let the flowers be. We also discovered ourselves face-to-face at my door as Zane prepared to go.

He cocked his head. "You know I won't settle for just one date with you, right?"

"Of course not," I said. "I'm irresistible."

"Then it won't surprise you if I do this."

He lowered his head and put his lips to mine, treating me to a warm and wonderful kiss. I hoped it would be the first of many to come. We'd not only captured a car thief together, but we'd captured each other's hearts.

*** *The End* ***

About the Author

     Diane Kelly is a former assistant state attorney general and tax advisor who spent much of her career fighting, or inadvertently working for, white-collar criminals. When she realized her experiences made great fodder for novels, her fingers hit the keyboard and thus began her Death & Taxes white-collar crime series. A proud graduate of her hometown's Citizens Police Academy, Diane is also the author of the Paw Enforcement K-9 series and the Busted motorcycle cop series. Her other series include the House Flipper cozy mystery series. She also writes romance and light contemporary fantasy stories. You can find Diane online at www.dianekelly.com, on her author page on Facebook, and on Twitter and Instagram at @DianeKellyBooks.

***

Dear Reader,

I hope you enjoyed this story as much as I enjoyed writing it for you!

What did you think of this book? Posting reviews online are a great way to share your thoughts with fellow readers and help each other find stories best suited to your individual tastes.

Be the first to hear about upcoming releases, special discounts, and subscriber-only perks by signing up for my newsletter at my website, www.DianeKelly.com. You can also find me online on my author page on Facebook. I'd love to connect with you on Twitter and Instagram, too! My Twitter and Instagram handle is @DianeKellyBooks.

I love to Skype with book clubs! Contact me via my website if you'd like to arrange a virtual visit with your group.

See the follow page for a list of my books, then read on for fun excerpts.

Happy reading! See you in the next story.

Diane

BOOKS BY DIANE KELLY

The Busted series:
Busted
Another Big Bust

The House Flipper series:
Dead as a Door Knocker
Dead in the Doorway

The Paw Enforcement series:
Paw Enforcement Bundle: Books 1-3 Plus Upholding the Paw
Novella (Discounted book bundle!)
Paw Enforcement
Paw and Order
Upholding the Paw (a bonus novella)
Laying Down the Paw
Against the Paw
Above the Paw
Enforcing the Paw
The Long Paw of the Law
Paw of the Jungle
Bending the Paw

The Tara Holloway Death & Taxes series:
Death, Taxes, and a French Manicure
Death, Taxes, and a Skinny No-Whip Latte
Death, Taxes, and Extra-Hold Hairspray
Death, Taxes, and a Sequined Clutch (a bonus novella)
Death, Taxes, and Peach Sangria
Death, Taxes, and Hot Pink Leg Warmers
Death, Taxes, and Green Tea Ice Cream
Death, Taxes, and Mistletoe Mayhem (a bonus novella)
Death, Taxes, and Silver Spurs
Death, Taxes, and Cheap Sunglasses

EXCERPTS

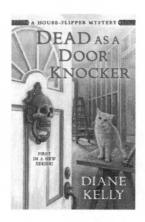

Dead as a Door Knocker – Excerpt

Chapter One
Deadbeats

Whitney Whitaker

I grabbed my purse, my tool belt, and the bright yellow hardhat I'd adorned with a chain of daisy decals. I gave my cat a kiss on the head. "Bye-bye, Sawdust." Looking into his baby blue eyes, I pointed a finger at him. "Be a good boy while mommy's at work, okay?"

The cat swiped at my finger with a paw the color of pine shavings. Given that my eyes and hair were the same shade as his, I could be taken for his mother if not for the fact that we were entirely different species. I'd adopted the furry runt after his mother, a stray, had given birth to him and two siblings in my uncle's barn. My cousins, Buck and Owen, had taken in the other two kittens, and my aunt and uncle gave the wayward mama cat a comfy home in their hilltop cabin on the Kentucky border.

After stepping outside, I turned around to lock the French doors that served as the entrance to my humble home. The place sat in my parents' backyard, on the far side of their kidney-shaped pool. In its former life, it had served as a combination pool house and garden shed. With the help of the contractors I'd befriended on my jobs, I'd converted the structure into a cozy guest house—the guest being yours truly. It had already been outfitted with a small three-quarter bath, so all we'd had to do was add a closet and kitchenette.

Furnishing a hundred and fifty square feet had been easy. There was room for only the bare essentials—a couple of bar stools at the kitchen counter, a twin bed and dresser, and a recliner that served as both a comfortable reading chair and a scratching post for Sawdust. Heaven forbid my sweet-but-spoiled cat sharpen his claws on the sisal post I'd bought him at the pet supply store. At least he enjoyed his carpet-covered cat tree. I'd positioned it by one of the windows that flanked the French doors. He passed his days on the highest perch, watching birds flitter about the birdhouses and feeders situated about the backyard.

At twenty-eight, I probably should've ventured farther from my parents' home by now. But the arrangement suited me and my parents just fine. They were constantly jetting off to Paris or Rome or some exotic locale I couldn't pronounce or find on a map if my life depended on it. Living here allowed me to keep an eye on their house and dog while they traveled, but the fact that we shared no walls gave us all some privacy. The arrangement also allowed me to sock away quite a bit of my earnings in savings. Soon, I'd be able to buy a house of my own. Not here in the Green Hills neighborhood, where real estate garnered a pretty penny. But maybe in one of the more affordable Nashville suburbs. While many young girls dreamed of beaded wedding gowns or palomino ponies, I'd dreamed of custom cabinets and and built-in bookshelves.

After locking the door, I turned to find my mother and her black-and-white Boston terrier, Yin-Yang, puttering around the backyard. Like me, Mom was blond, though she now needed the help of her hairdresser to keep the stray grays at bay. Like Yin-Yang, Mom was petite, standing only five feet three inches. Mom was still in her pink bathrobe, a steaming mug of coffee in her hand. While she helped with billing at my dad's otolaryngology practice, she normally went in late and left early. Her part-time schedule allowed her to avoid traffic, gave her time take care of things around the house and spend time with her precious pooch.

"Good morning!" I called.

My mother returned the sentiment, while Yin-Yang raised her two-tone head and replied with a cheerful *Arf-arf!* The bark scared off a trio of finches who'd been indulging in a breakfast of assorted seeds at a nearby feeder.

Mom stepped over, the dog trotting along with her, staring up at me with its adorable little bug eyes. "You're off early," Mom said, a hint of question in her voice.

No sense telling her I was on my way to an eviction. She already thought my job was beneath me. She assumed working as a property manager involved constantly dealing with deadbeats and clogged toilets. Truth be told, much of my job did involve delinquent tenants or backed-up plumbing. But there was much more to it than that. Helping landlords turn rundown real estate into attractive residences, helping hopeful tenants locate the perfect place for their particular needs, making sure everything ran smoothly for everyone involved. I considered myself to be in the homemaking business. But rather than try, for the umpteenth time, to explain myself, I simply said, "I've got a busy day."

Mom tilted her head. "Too busy to study for your real estate exam?"

I fought the urge to groan. As irritating as my mother could be, she only wanted the best for me. Problem was, we didn't agree on what the best was. Instead of starting an argument I said, "Don't worry. The test isn't for another couple of weeks. I've still got plenty of time."

"Okay," she acquiesced, the two syllables soaked in skepticism. "Have a good day, sweetie." At least those five words sounded sincere.

"You, too, Mom." I reached down and ruffled the dog's ears. "Bye, girl."

I made my way to the picket fence that enclosed the backyard and let myself out of the gate and onto the driveway. After tossing my hard hat and tool belt into the passenger seat of my red Honda CR-V, I swapped out the magnetic WHITAKER WOODWORKING sign on the door for one that read HOME & HEARTH REALTY. Yep, I wore two hats. The hard hat when moonlighting as a carpenter for my uncle, and a metaphorical second hat when working my day job as a property manager for a real estate business. This morning, I sported the metaphorical hat as I headed up Hillsboro Pike into Nashville. Fifteen minutes later, I turned onto Sweetbriar Avenue. In the driveway of the house on the corner sat a shiny midnight blue Infiniti Q70L sedan with vanity plates that read TGENTRY. My shackles rose at the sight.

Thaddeus Gentry III owned Gentry Real Estate Development, Inc. or, as I called it, GREED Incorporated. Okay, so I'd added an extra E to make the spelling work. Still, it was true. The guy was as money-hungry and ruthless as they come. He was singlehandedly responsible for the gentrification of several old Nashville neighborhoods. While gentrification wasn't necessarily a bad thing—after all it rid the city of ramshackle houses in dire need of repairs—Thad Gentry took advantage of homeowners, offering them pennies on the dollar, knowing they couldn't afford the increase in property taxes that would result as their modest neighborhoods transformed into upscale communities. He'd harass holdouts by reporting any city code violations, no matter how minor. He also formed homeowners' associations in the newly renovated neighborhoods, and ensured the HOA put pressure on the remaining original residents to bring their houses up to snuff. These unfortunate folks found they no longer felt at home and usually gave in and moved on . . . to where, who knows?

When I'd come by a week ago in a final attempt to collect from the tenants, I'd noticed a for sale sign in the yard where Thad Gentry's car was parked. The sign was gone now. *Had Gentry bought the property? Had he set his sights on the neighborhood?*

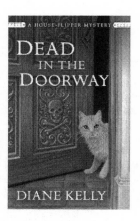

Dead in the Doorway - Excerpt

Chapter One
Peanut Butter and Jealousy

Whitney Whitaker

Knock-knock.

My fluffy cat Sawdust raised his head from the sofa and eyed the door. Curious to see who had come by, he hopped down from the furniture and followed me as I walked to the door and pulled it open.

Nashville might sit in the south, but winters here could nonetheless be quite frigid. My cousin Buck stood on the porch, blowing into his cupped hands to warm them, his shoulders hunched inside his heavy winter coat. Given that our fathers were brothers, Buck and I shared the last name Whitaker. We also shared a tall physique, blue eyes, and hair the color of unfinished pine. But while Buck sported a full beard, a monthly waxing at the beauty salon kept any would-be whiskers away from my face.

As half owner of the stone cottage I called home, Buck could have let himself in with his key. But he was polite enough to respect the privacy of me and my two roommates, Colette and Emmalee. I waved him in. "You're just in time for lunch."

"Looks like I timed my arrival perfectly."

After stepping inside, he removed his coat and hung it on a hook near the door. He reached down and gave my cat a pat on the head. "Hey, boy."

Sawdust offered a *mew* in return.

The cat trotted along with us as Buck followed me to the kitchen. My best friend, Colette Chevalier, stood at the counter preparing warm sandwiches on her panini press. Colette had adorable dark curls and a bright smile, somehow managing to remain thin despite working in the restaurant at the Hermitage Hotel in downtown Nashville. I was jealous. Thanks to her irresistible cooking, I'd gained five pounds since we'd moved in together.

The two of us had been best friends since we'd gone pot luck for roommates in the freshman dormitory at Middle Tennessee State University and been assigned to live together. We'd hit if off right away. While some of the other girls spent their weekends at parties or nightclubs, loud crowds weren't our style. Not that we weren't fun-loving. Colette and I often hosted small gatherings in our room at the dorm and watched movies, made crafts, or played board games with friends. We'd even started a monthly book club. We'd pool our spare change for snacks, and Colette would prepare simple yet delicious appetizers for the group.

After we'd graduated, Colette had followed me up the road to my hometown of Nashville. While she'd gone on to complete a culinary arts program, I'd continued to help out at Whitaker Woodworking, my Uncle Roger's carpentry business. I'd also landed a part-time job as a property manager for Home & Hearth, a mom-and-pop real estate firm. Colette liked to feed people, and I liked to house them. We were both domestic goddesses, in our own right.

Colette cut a glance at my cousin. "Here to mooch a meal, Buck?"

"It's only fair." He plunked himself down on one of the stools at the breakfast bar. "After all, I installed all those lights under the cabinets, like you asked me to. Never asked for nothing in return, neither."

"You got me there." She slid the sandwich she'd made for me onto a plate, cut it diagonally, and set it down in front of me. She used the knife to point to the variety of breads, cheeses, and meats next to the press. "What'll it be, Buck?"

"How about a peanut butter and jelly?"

She brandished the knife and gave him a look that was as pointed as her kitchen tool. "I am a professional chef. Would you ask Harry Connick, Jr. to sing 'Yankee Doodle?'"

A mischievous grin played about Buck's mouth. "Surprise me."

As Colette set about making Buck's sandwich, I inquired about her late return home the night before. The restaurant closed at 10:00, and she normally arrived home around midnight after working a late shift. But it had been after 2:00 when she came through our front door last night. I knew because I'd stayed up late in my bedroom binge-watching home renovation shows. *What can I say? I'm addicted to them.* "You were late getting home last night. Problems at the restaurant?"

She seemed to stiffen, and hesitated before replying. "No, no problems." She added another slice of cheese to Buck's sandwich and closed the press.

I picked up one of the halves of my warm panini. "Let me guess. You finally had that glass of wine the sommelier has been begging you to drink with him."

Buck straightened in his seat next to me. "The sommelier's been hitting on you? That's harassment. You should turn him in."

"He's not in my chain of command," Colette said. "He's just a coworker. Besides, I'd hardly call his behavior harassment. All he did was ask if I'd like to sample a rare vintage he'd bought."

Buck's eyes narrowed. "You and who else?"

"Only me. He knew I'd appreciate it. It was a two-hundred-dollar bottle of burgundy. A 2008 *Domaine Leflaive Puligny-Montrachet Les Folatières 1er Cru*."

Having been born and raised in New Orleans, Colette's French was impeccable. Buck's attempt to speak the language, on the other hand, was downright embarrassing.

"La-di-da," he said. "Mercy boo-coos."

"How was the wine?" I asked.

Colette kissed her fingertips. *"Magnifique."*

Buck scowled. *Could he be jealous?* My cousin and best friend got along well, even ribbed each other on regular basis, but I'd never considered that either of them might be interested in something more than friendship. His reaction told me that maybe I'd been naïve. Then again, Buck was old-fashioned, a southern gentleman. He could be simply looking out for Colette.

"I thought I smelled something cooking." Our third roommate, Emmalee, entered the kitchen, still in her pajamas despite the fact that it was half past one in the afternoon. Her coppery hair was pulled up in wild pile on top of her head. She rubbed her eyes with her freckled hands, looking only half awake.

Buck lifted his chin in greeting. "Hey there, Raggedy Ann."

"Hey, Buck." She turned her attention to Colette. "What're you making?"

"Paninis," Colette said as she lifted the top of the device. "Want one?"

Emmalee slid onto a stool next to my cousin. "Do you even have to ask?"

Emmalee was a nursing student in her early twenties, seven years younger than Colette and I. She worked as a waitress at the same fancy restaurant where Colette served as a chef. That's where they'd met. The three of us had become roommates only a few short weeks ago. Colette had broken up with her long-term boyfriend and needed a new place to live. Emmalee's previous roommate got a job transfer and left her looking for a new living arrangement. I'd been living like a hobbit in the converted pool house behind my parents' house, and it had been high time for me to get a place of my own.

Although Buck and I had originally planned to flip this place, we'd decided it made more sense for me to move in rather than put it on the market. I'd invited Colette and Emmalee to share the house with me. The three of us got along great. Colette did the grocery shopping and cooking, Emmalee did most of the indoor cleaning, and I made repairs and maintained the lawn. From each according to her ability, as well as one-third of the utilities.

Colette set Buck's plate in front of him. "Eat up, big boy."

He picked up the sandwich, took a bite, and moaned in bliss.

Colette smiled. "I take it you like the surprise?"

He nodded and rubbed his tummy as he chewed. She sauntered over to the fridge, retrieved a pitcher of sweet tea, and poured him a glass to go along with it. With Buck all set, she proceeded to prepare a sandwich for Emmalee.

Emmalee turned toward me and Buck, and ran her gaze over our work boots and coveralls. "Y'all got a carpentry job today?"

I'd spent the morning at one of the properties Home & Hearth managed, replacing a couple of rotten boards on the back deck. Buck had been helping his father and his younger brother Owen build a custom entertainment center at a house in Nolensville. But after lunch, we planned to head over to a property I'd just purchased with the help of Marv and Wanda Hartley, the owners of Home & Hearth. The Hartleys were a kind, down-to-earth couple nearing retirement age. They'd known Buck and I were looking for a property to flip, and they realized the fixer-upper on a quiet, established cul-de-sac could be the perfect project for us. They'd not only brought the listing to my attention, but had also made me a loan at a ridiculously low interest rate so I could afford to buy the place. I couldn't ask for better bosses.

"I'm going to show Buck the place I bought," I explained to Emmalee. "In just a few weeks, when we put it up for sale, we'll net a nice profit." I rubbed my hands together greedily.

Buck was more cautious. "Best not count our chickens before they're hatched."

He was being a party pooper, but he had a point. Flipping houses was a risky business. Sometimes what started as a minor renovation could turn into a major overhaul, depending on what troubles a house might have hidden. What's more, the real estate market was subject to wide fluctuations. Properties could go up or down in value virtually overnight. But Buck and I knew good and well what we were getting ourselves into. Both of us were willing to take a chance. We might not be able to count on much in this business, but we could always count on each other.

When we finished our lunch, we thanked Colette and offered to clean up the kitchen before we left.

"I got it," she said. "No worries. But before you go, I've got something for you, Whitney."

"What is it?"

Colette went to a shopping bag on the counter, dipped her hand into the bag, and dug around. When she pulled her hand out, it was clutching a small pink canister with a metal ring on the end. "Pepper spray." She pressed the device into my hand. "You never know when a crazy tenant might come after you again."

People tended to get angry when they were evicted. One such irate tenant had come after me recently. It couldn't hurt to have a means of defense at the ready. "Thanks, Colette. I'll attach it to my keychain."

Buck and I headed for the door. Before we left, I grabbed Sawdust's carrier and harness so he could come take a look at the house, too. Between the carpentry work, the property management gig, and working on flip houses, I wasn't home much. I felt guilty leaving my cat alone for long stretches of time. I missed him, and I assumed he missed me. Besides, cats were instinctual explorers, furry and four-footed Davy Crocketts or Daniel Boones, Lewis and Clark with mews and claws. He'd have some fun exploring the flip house.

Chapter Two
Grand Tour

Whitney Whitaker

Click. Click-click.

My breath fogged in the frigid air as I stood on the cracked concrete driveway and snapped cell phone pics of the dilapidated white Colonial. Later, I'd look the pictures over and make a list of the repairs to be done and the materials needed.

From off to our right came the muted rumble of an airplane engine as a Delta flight took off from the Nashville airport, aiming for the heavens. Plane traffic was to be expected in the Donelson neighborhood that bordered the BNA property. Fortunately, this house was far enough away that the sound amounted to nothing more than white noise, hardly noticeable. In fact, the home's easy access to the airport, Percy Priest Reservoir, and the Gaylord Opryland hotel and shopping mall would be selling points when we put it on the market. The fact that the house sat atop a small slope, offering a view of the downtown skyline, was another plus. The outer suburbs might have newer homes, but they didn't offer the Donelson neighborhood's convenience.

Sawdust performed figure eights between my legs, wrapping his leash tightly around my ankles as if he were a cowboy at the rodeo and I was a calf he'd roped. I slid my phone into the pocket of my coveralls, leaned down to extricate my legs from the tangled leash, and picked up my cat before turning to my cousin. "What do you think?"

Buck's narrowed gaze roamed over the structure, taking in the peeling paint, the weathered boards, and the missing balusters on the front porch railing. Several shutters had gone AWOL, too. A wooden trellis stretched up the side of the house, looking like an oversized skeleton trying to scale the roof. Several of its slats hung askew, like broken ribs. The climbing roses that graced the trellis had withered in the winter weather, awaiting their annual spring rejuvenation.

Buck cocked his head as he continued his visual inspection. "We've got our work cut out for us. But I don't see anything we can't handle."

The home's former owner, a widow named Lillian Walsh, had lived a long and happy life here before passing from natural causes. Her fixed income hadn't allowed for much upkeep, though, and her two sons had put the place on the market as-is rather than deal with the cost and hassle of repairs. That's where flippers like me and my cousin came in.

House flippers maximize their profits by investing both their money and sweat equity in their properties, fixing up the homes themselves rather than hiring the work out at a markup. As a professional carpenter, Buck had the know-how to spruce the place up. Having regularly helped out at Whitaker Woodworking over the years, I'd grown adept at carpentry, too. What's more, thanks to my property management work and YouTube tutorials, I'd learned how to handle all sorts of minor repairs. If you need drywall patched or a sticky door re-hung, I'm your gal.

Looking back at the house, I felt hopeful. *A new year means a new beginning, doesn't it?* There was no better way to start a new year than by renovating a house. I motioned for Buck to follow me. "C'mon. I'll show you the inside."

We ascended the crumbling brick steps to the porch. A bristly doormat that read WELCOME lay in front of the door, directly greeting us and more subtly inviting us to wipe our feet. A yellow door-hanger style advertisement for an income tax preparation service hung from the doorknob, the business proprietor attempting to get an early jump on the competition. A two-foot tall ceramic frog with a fly on his unfurled tongue stood next to the door, his bulbous eyes seeming to stare at us. I could understand why the frog was smiling—he was about to enjoy a snack. But why the tiny fly was smiling was beyond me. He seemed clueless about his fate.

"Fancy door," Buck said as he stopped before it.

Indeed, it was. The door was made of heavy, solid wood with

an ornate oval of frosted glass to let in light yet provide some measure of privacy. Once it was sanded and treated to a new coat of glossy paint, it would really add to the curb appeal. "Maybe we should consider painting it red. Add a splash of color to the place."

"Not a bad idea."

Setting Sawdust down on the porch, I unlocked the door and the three of us stepped inside, stopping on the landing of the split-level house. The landing's mock-tile linoleum featured small squares in a lovely shade of lima bean green that had been popular back when disco was the rage and a loaf of bread cost thirty-six cents. But at least the steps were real hardwood.

To the right of the landing was a coat closet with a rickety folding door that was either half closed or half open, depending on how you looked at it. But optimist or pessimist, you couldn't miss the smell of mothballs coming from inside. So many dusty jackets and coats were squeezed into the closet that the rod bent under the weight, threatening to break. The outerwear shared the lower space with a mangled umbrella and a hefty Kirby vacuum cleaner circa 1965, complete with attachments. The shelf above sagged under the weight of a reel-to-reel home movie projector, around which mismatched mittens, scarves, and knit caps had been stuffed. Lillian's family had cleared the house of everything of value, leaving the worthless junk behind for the buyer—*yours truly*—to deal with. *Sigh.*

After closing the front door behind us, I unclipped the leash from Sawdust's harness, setting him free to explore. Noting that the house felt warmer than expected, I checked the thermostat mounted next to the closet. It read 72. *That's odd. Didn't I turn it down to 60 the last time I was here?* I hoped I'd merely forgotten to adjust it when I'd left. I'd hate to think the HVAC system might be on the fritz.

I reached out and gave the lever a downward nudge. The three of us wouldn't be here long. No sense paying for heat nobody would be needing.

The thermostat adjusted, I swept my arm, inviting Buck to proceed me upstairs. "After you, partner."

We ascended the steps with Sawdust trotting ahead of us. On the way, Buck grasped both the wall-mounted railing and the wrought-iron banister and gave each of them a hearty yank, testing them for safety. While the banister checked out, the wooden rail mounted to the wall jiggled precariously. One glance at the support brackets told us why.

"It's got some loose screws," Buck said. "Just like you."

I rolled my eyes. "Ha-ha."

He circled a finger in the air. "Put it on the list."

"Will do." I pulled my phone from my pocket and snapped a photo of the loose bracket as a reminder to myself.

As we topped the stairs, Buck came to a screeching halt, one work boot hovering over the carpet as he refused to step on it. "Yuck."

Couldn't say that I blamed him. The carpet was hideous, a worn shag in the same greenish-brown hue as the hairballs Sawdust occasionally coughed up. Ripping out the carpet would give us no small pleasure. But I wasn't about to let some ugly, balding carpet spoil my enthusiasm. I gave my cousin a push, forcing him forward. "Go on, you wimp. It's not going to reach up and grab you."

"You sure about that?"

To our left, the living and dining areas formed a rectangle that ran from the front to the back of the house. The master bedroom and bath mirrored the layout to the right. In the center sprawled the wide kitchen.

"Wait 'til you see this!" I circled around Buck and pushed open the swinging saloon doors that led into the space.

Buck proceeded through them and stopped in the center of the kitchen to gape. "What is this place? A portal back to 1970?"

Between the harvest gold appliances, the rust-orange countertops and the globe pendant light hanging from a loopy chain, it appeared as if we'd time-traveled back to a much groovier era. But while the kitchen was hopelessly out of date, it was also wonderfully spacious. Plus, the cabinets would be salvageable if the outdated scalloped valances over the sink and stove were removed.

"Replacing the appliances and countertops is a no-brainer," I said. "But look at all this space! And the cabinets just need re-facing. They're solid wood. That'll save us time and money."

Buck stepped over and rapped his knuckles on the door of a cabinet. *Rap-rap.* Satisfied by the feel and sound, he nodded in agreement.

The counters bore an array of Lillian's cooking implements, including a ceramic pitcher repurposed to hold utensils. Cutting boards in a variety of shapes and sizes leaned against the backsplash. A recipe box stood between an ancient toaster and a blender. A quaint collection of antique food tins graced the top of a wooden bread box. Hershey's cocoa. Barnum's Animal Crackers. Arm & Hammer Baking Soda.

As Buck and Sawdust took a peek at the plumbing under the sink, I walked over to the end of the cabinets and spread my arms. "Let's add an L-shaped extension here." An extension would increase the counter space and storage and, after all, kitchen renovations were the most profitable rehab investment.

Without bothering to look up, Buck agreed. "Okey doke."

My cousin and I had an implicit understanding. He left the design details up to me, while I gave him control over the structural aspects of the renovations.

While he continued his inspection, I meandered around the kitchen, snapping several more pictures before stopping at the fridge. A dozen blue ribbons were affixed with magnets to the refrigerator door, proudly proclaiming Lillian Walsh as the baker of the "Best Peach Pie" and "Best Peach Cobbler" at various fairs and festivals throughout the state. With my cooking skills, I'd be lucky to earn a participation ribbon.

A hutch on the adjacent wall was loaded with more cookbooks than I could count. I eased over to take a closer look. One book was devoted entirely to potato recipes, another to casseroles. A quick glimpse inside a few of the books told me the recipes were as likely to clog the arteries as fill the tummy. Some of them sounded darn delicious, though. I returned the books to the shelf and turned to find Sawdust traipsing along the countertop while Buck peered into the drawers.

My cousin pulled out what appeared to be a caulking gun, along with a heavy metal lever-like tool with a rubber-coated handle. The latter resembled an airplane throttle. He held them up for me to see. "What the heck are these gadgets for?"

"You're asking the wrong person." While I loved working *on* kitchens, I didn't particularly like working *in* them once they were complete. Boxed mac-and-cheese marked the pinnacle of my culinary skills.

"Let's have Colette take a look," he suggested. "She might could use some of these things."

While Colette already had an extensive complement of kitchen equipment, this room contained items that probably hadn't been produced in half a century or more. If nothing else, she'd find these artifacts intriguing.

Having fully explored the kitchen, Buck and I moved on to the master bedroom. Like the kitchen, the room was dated but spacious. The walls bore peeling wallpaper in a flocked fleur-de-lis pattern. Only the bed and a night table remained, all other furniture having been removed from the room. A stack of books towered on the night table, some hardcover, some paperbacks. Sawdust hopped up onto the bed to inspect the random items that had been placed there. Several pairs of ladies' shoes. A stack of Sunday dresses still on the hangers. A small jewelry box. A quick peek inside told me it contained only a few pieces of what I assumed to be cheap costume jewelry. I let Sawdust take a quick and curious sniff before closing the lid.

We continued into the master bath, which featured a once-fashionable pink porcelain tub, toilet, and sink. Wallpaper in a gaudy yet charming rose pattern adorned the walls. Fresh, if faded, towels filled the under-sink cabinet, along with an assortment of medications and beauty products. A tin box sat next to the sink. The top was open, revealing a trio of pink soaps in the shape and scent of roses. As we looked around, Sawdust leapt up onto the edge of the tub and circumnavigated it with the ease and agility of a tightrope walker.

I snapped a pic before turning to Buck. "Let's replace that old bathtub with a walk-in shower, and add a jetted garden tub over there." I pointed to an open space under the window.

He pulled out a measuring tape to size up the space and, satisfied the tub would fit, issued an "mm-hmm" of agreement.

Having completed the tour of the master suite, we made a quick pass through the living and dining rooms, which contained a slouchy velveteen sofa, a framed still life painting depicting a bowl of assorted fruit, and a glass-top coffee table that bore the sticky tell-tale fingerprints of spoiled grandchildren. A small wooden box sat atop the table. The box was intricately engraved with hearts, diamonds, spades, and clubs along the sides, and a fancy letter W on the lid. The lid was open, revealing two yellowed decks of playing cards nestled inside. The cards rested face up, the two jokers at the top of the decks grinning wickedly up at me as if they shared a sinister secret. Sawdust seized the opportunity to sharpen his claws on the couch before following us downstairs.

Creak. Creak. The bottom step complained under my weight, then Buck's. *Looks like we've got a loose tread.* Sawdust stepped soundlessly down, too light to elicit a response.

Other than a rusty washer and dry set and a couple of wire hangers on a rod, the laundry room was empty. The guest bedroom contained a full-sized bed covered in a crocheted afghan and a basic bureau with three empty cans of Budweiser sitting atop it. They appeared to be only the latest in a long series of beers enjoyed in the bed, as evidenced by a pattern of ring stains roughly resembling the Olympic symbol. I wondered who Lillian's beer-guzzling guest had been.

The other bedroom had been converted to a sewing room and appeared untouched. A white Singer sewing machine sat on a table, while a bookshelf to the right sported a selection of thread and rickrack, as well as a pincushion in the quintessential tomato motif. A plastic box filled with spare, shiny buttons sat open on one of the shelves like a miniature treasure chest filled with gold. Swatches of fabric draped over a quilt rack.

After a quick trip to the garage, the tour was complete. The bottom step creaked again as we made our way back up to the front doorway. There, I shared my overall vision for the house. "Classic black and white tile in the baths and kitchen. Paint in robin's egg blue for the walls." The look would be neutral and timeless, and would tie in well with the exterior colors. "Black hardwood floors would be a nice complement, too."

"Works for me," Buck said.

After noting that the thermostat reading was on its way down, I patted my leg and called for my cat to meet us on the landing. "Sawdust! Here, boy!" When Sawdust trotted up the steps, I reattached his leash to his harness and we headed out the door into the gathering winter dusk. With my hands full of keys and the cat's leash, I left the tax-preparation ad hanging from the knob to be dealt with later. Buck and I agreed to meet at the house at noon the following day to take measurements and start on the demolition. House flippers don't take weekends off.

Buck raised a hand out the window of his van as he backed out of the driveway and drove off. I looked up at the house one more time, feeling heartened and hopeful. *Yep. A fresh start.*

Paw Enforcement - Excerpt

Chapter One - Job Insecurity

Fort Worth Police Officer Megan Luz

My rusty-haired partner lay convulsing on the hot asphalt, his jaw clenching and his body involuntarily curling into a jittery fetal position as two probes delivered 1,500 volts of electricity to his groin. The crotch of his police-issue trousers darkened as he lost control of his bladder.

I'd never felt close to my partner in the six months we'd worked together, but at that particular moment I sensed a strong bond. The connection likely stemmed from the fact that we were indeed connected then--by the two wires leading from the Taser in my hand to my partner's twitching testicles.

#

I didn't set out to become a hero. I decided on a career in law enforcement for three other reasons:

1) Having been a twirler in my high school's marching band, I knew how to handle a baton.

2) Other than barking short orders or rattling off Miranda rights, working as a police officer wouldn't require me to talk much.

3) I had an excess of pent-up anger. Might as well put it to good use,

right?

Of course I didn't plan to be a street cop forever. Just long enough to work my way up to detective. A lofty goal, but I knew I could do it--even if nobody else did.

I'd enjoyed my studies in criminal justice at Sam Houston State University in Hunstville, Texas, especially the courses in criminal psychology. No, I'm not some sick, twisted creep who gets off on hearing about criminals who steal, rape, and murder. I just thought that if we could figure out why criminals do bad things, maybe we could stop them, you know?

To supplement my student loans, I'd worked part-time at the gift shop in the nearby state prison museum, selling tourists such quality souvenirs as ceramic ash trays made by the prisoners or decks of cards containing prison trivia. The unit had once been home to Clyde Barrow of Bonnie and Clyde fame and was also the site of an eleven-day siege in 1974 spearheaded by heroin kingpin Fredrick Gomez Carrasco, jailed for killing a police officer. Our top-selling item was a child's time-out chair fashioned after Old Sparky, the last remaining electric chair used in Texas. Talk about cruel and unusual punishment.

TO THE CORNER, LITTLE BILLY.

NO, MOMMY, NO! ANYTHING BUT THE CHAIR!

I'd looked forward to becoming a cop, keeping the streets safe for citizens, maintaining law and order, promoting civility and justice. Such noble ideals, right?

What I hadn't counted on was that I'd be working with a force full of macho shitheads. With my uncanny luck, I'd been assigned to partner with the most macho, most shit-headed cop of all, Derek the "Big Dick" Mackey. As implied in the aforementioned reference to twitching testicles, our partnership had not ended well.

That's why I was sitting here outside the chief's office in a cheap plastic chair, chewing my thumbnail down to a painful nub, waiting to find out whether I still had a job. Evidently, Tasering your partner in the COJONES is considered not only an overreaction, but also a blatant violation of department policy, one which carried the potential penalty of dismissal from the force, not to mention a criminal assault charge.

So much for those noble ideals, huh?

I ran a finger over my upper lip, blotting the nervous sweat that had formed there. Would I be booted off the force after only six months on duty?

With the city's budget crisis, there'd been threats of cutbacks and layoffs across the board. No department would be spared. If the chief had to fire anyone, he'd surely start with the rookie with the Irish temper. If the chief canned me, what would I do? My aspirations of becoming a detective would go down the toilet. Once again I'd be Megan Luz, a.k.a. "The Loser." As you've probably guessed, my pent-up anger had a lot to do with that nickname.

I pulled my telescoping baton from my belt and flicked my wrist to extend it. SNAP! Though my police baton had a different feel from the twirling baton I'd used in high school, I'd quickly learned that with a few minor adjustments to accommodate the distinctive weight distribution I could perform many of the same tricks with it. I began to work the stick, performing a basic flat spin. The repetitive motion calmed me, helped me think. It was like a twirling metal stress ball. SWISH-SWISH-SWISH.

The chief's door opened and three men exited. All wore navy tees emblazoned with white letters spelling BOMB SQUAD stretched tight across well-developed pecs. Though the bomb squad was officially part of the Fort Worth Fire Department, the members worked closely with the police. Where there's a bomb, there's a crime, after all. Most likely these men were here to discuss safety procedures for the upcoming Concerts in the Park. After what happened at the Boston marathon, extra precautions were warranted for large public events.

The guy in front, a blond with a military-style haircut, cut his eyes my way. He watched me spin my baton for a moment, then dipped his head in acknowledgement when my gaze met his. He issued the standard southern salutation. "Hey."

His voice was deep with a subtle rumble, like far-off thunder warning of an oncoming storm. The guy wasn't tall, but he was broad-shouldered, muscular, and undeniably masculine. He had dark green eyes and a dimple in his chin that drew my eyes downward, over his soft, sexy mouth, and back up again.

A hot flush exploded through me. I tried to nod back at him, but my muscles seemed to have atrophied. My hand stopped moving and clutched my baton in a death grip. All I could do was watch as he and the other men continued into the hall and out of sight.

BLURGH. Acting like a frigid virgin. How humiliating!

Once the embarrassment waned, I began to wonder. Had the bomb squad guy found me attractive? Is that why he'd greeted me? Or was he simply being friendly to a fellow public servant?

My black locks were pulled back in a tight, torturous bun, a style that enabled me to look professional on the force while allowing me to retain my feminine allure after hours. There were only so many sacrifices I was willing to make for employment and my long, lustrous hair was not one of them. My freckles showed through my light makeup. Hard to feel like a tough cop if you're wearing too much foundation or more than one coat of mascara. Fortunately, I had enough natural coloring to get by with little in the way of cosmetics. I was a part Irish-American, part Mexican-American mutt, with just enough Cherokee blood to give me an instinctive urge to dance in the rain but not enough to qualify me for any college scholarships. My figure was neither thin nor voluptuous, but my healthy diet and regular exercise kept me in decent shape. It was entirely possible that the guy had been checking me out. Right?

I mentally chastised myself. CHILL, MEGAN. I hadn't had a date since I'd joined the force, but so what? I had more important things to deal with at the moment. I collapsed my baton, returned it to my belt, and took a deep breath to calm my nerves.

The chief's secretary, a middle-aged brunette wearing a poly-blend dress, sat at her desk typing a report into the computer. She had twice as much butt as chair, her thighs draping over the sides of the seat. But who could blame her? Judging from the photos on her desk, she'd squeezed out three children in rapid succession. Having grown up in a family of five kids, I knew mothers had little time to devote to themselves when their kids were young and constantly needed mommy to feed them, clean up their messes, and bandage their various boo-boos. She wore no jewelry, no makeup, and no nail polish. The chief deserved credit for not hiring a younger, prettier, better accessorized woman for the job. Obviously, she'd been hired for her mad office skills. She'd handled a half dozen phone calls in the short time I'd been waiting and her fingers moved over the keyboard at such a speedy pace it was a miracle her hands didn't burst into flame. Whatever she was being paid, it wasn't enough.

The woman's phone buzzed again and she punched her intercom button. "Yessir?" She paused a moment. "I'll send her in." She hung up the phone and turned to me. "The chief is ready for you."

"Thanks." I stood on wobbly legs.

Would the chief take my badge today? Was my career in law enforcement over?

Death, Taxes, and a French Manicure - Excerpt

Chapter One

Some People Just Need Shooting

When I was nine, I formed a Silly Putty pecker for my Ken doll, knowing he'd have no chance of fulfilling Barbie's needs given the permanent state of erectile dysfunction with which the toy designers at Mattel had cursed him. I knew a little more about sex than most girls, what with growing up in the country and all. The first time I saw our neighbor's Black Angus bull mount an unsuspecting heifer, my two older brothers explained it all to me.

"He's getting him some," they'd said.

"Some what?" I'd asked.

"Nookie."

We watched through the barbed wire fence until the strange ordeal was over. Frankly, the process looked somewhat uncomfortable for the cow, who continued to chew her cud throughout the entire encounter. But when the bull dismounted, nuzzled her chin, and wandered away, I swore I saw a smile on that cow's face and a look of quiet contentment in her eyes. She was in love.

I'd been in search of that same feeling for myself ever since.

My partner and I had spent the afternoon huddled at a cluttered desk in the back office of an auto parts store perusing the owner's financial records, searching for evidence of tax fraud. Yeah, you got me. I work for the IRS. Not exactly the kind of career that makes a person popular at cocktail parties. But those brave enough to get to know me learn I'm actually a nice person, fun even, and they have nothing to fear. I have better things to do than nickel and dime taxpayers whose worst crime was inflating the value of the Glen Campbell albums they donated to Goodwill.

"I'll be right back, Tara." My partner smoothed the front of his starched white button-down as he stood from the folding chair. Eddie Bardin was tall, lean, and African-American, but having been raised in the upper-middle-class, predominately white Dallas suburbs, he had a hard time connecting to his roots. He'd had nothing to overcome, unless you counted his affinity for Phil Collins' music, Heineken beer, and khaki chinos, tastes which he had yet to conquer. Eddie was more L.L. Bean than L.L. Cool J.

I nodded to Eddie and tucked an errant strand of my chestnut hair behind my ear. Turning back to the spreadsheet in front of me, I flicked aside the greasy burger and onion ring wrappers the store's owner, Jack Battaglia, had left on the desk after lunch. I couldn't make heads or tails out of the numbers on the page. Battaglia didn't know jack about keeping books and, judging from his puny salaries account, he'd been too cheap to hire a professional.

A few seconds after Eddie left the room, the door to the office banged open. Battaglia loomed in the doorway, his husky body filling the narrow space. He wore a look of purpose and his store's trademark bright green jumpsuit, the cheerful color at odds with the open box cutter clutched in his furry-knuckled fist.

"Hey!" Instinctively, I leapt from my seat, the metal chair falling over behind me and clanging to the floor.

Battaglia lunged at me. My heart whirled in my chest. There was no time to pull my gun. The best I could do was throw out my right arm to deflect his attempt to plunge the blade into my jugular. The sharp blade slid across my forearm, just above my wrist, but with so much adrenaline rocketing through my system, I felt no immediate pain. If not for the blood seeping through the sleeve of my navy nylon raid jacket, I wouldn't have even known I'd been cut. Underneath was my favorite pink silk blouse, a coup of a find on the clearance rack at Neiman Marcus Last Call, now sliced open, the blood-soaked material gaping to reveal a short but deep gash.

My jaw clamped tighter than a chastity belt on a pubescent princess. This jerk was going down.

My block had knocked him to the side. Taking advantage of our relative positioning, I threw a roundhouse kick to Battaglia's stomach, my steel-toed cherry-red Doc Martens sinking into his soft paunch. The shoes were the perfect combination of utility and style, another great find at a two-for-one sale at the Galleria.

The kick didn't take the beer-bellied bastard out of commission, but at least it sent him backwards a few feet, putting a little more distance between us. A look of surprise flashed across Battaglia's face as he stumbled backward. He clearly hadn't expected a skinny, five-foot-two-inch bookish woman to put up such a fierce fight. Neener-neener.

Made in the USA
San Bernardino, CA
16 May 2020